A King Production presents…

Baller Bitches
VOLUME 5
FULL CIRCLE

A NOVEL

JOY DEJA KING

ISBN 13: 978-1-958834-82-4
ISBN 10: 1-958834-82-3
Cover concept by Joy Deja King

Library of Congress Cataloging-in-Publication Data;
King, Deja Joy
Baller Bitches Volume 5: a series/by Joy Deja King
For complete Library of Congress Copyright info visit;
www.joydejaking.com Twitter: @joydejaking

A King Production
P.O. Box 912, Collierville, TN 38027

A King Production and the above portrayal log are trademarks of A King Production LLC

Dedication

This Book is Dedicated To My:

Family, Readers and Supporters.
I LOVE you guys so much. Please believe that!!

There Is No Force
More Powerful Than A
Woman
Determined
To Rise...

~ Dorothy Dandridge ~

Dear Readers:

We have officially come to the end of the Baller Bitches Series and honestly I feel so sad. I've grown somewhat attached to the characters Diamond, Kennedy and Blair. All these women have characteristics that I see in my own girlfriends or myself...the good ones and the flaws ☺ With that being said, I hope you all enjoy this final chapter in the series and I truly appreciate you all going on this journey with these ladies and me.

Much Love,

Joy Deja King

A KING PRODUCTION

Baller

Bitches

VOLUME 5
FULL
CIRCLE

A Novel

JOY DEJA KING

Chapter One

The Comeback Queens

Diamond was rooted to the ground, her knees pressed into the damp cemetery grass as her mother's casket was slowly lowered into the earth. The heavy gray sky mirrored the somber mood of the attendees, all dressed in black. Cameron and Kirk stood several feet away, deep in conversation. Neither man noticed the subtle movement in the crowd—a trio of men blending into the sea of black. Diamond, however, was hyper-aware. Men wearing black baseball caps with a bandana around their mouth caught her attention. They weren't mourning. They were watching.

Diamond's breath hitched and her heart slammed against her ribcage when one of the men reached into the waistband of his pants and pulled out the unmistakable shape of a gun, her eyes locked onto the glint of steel in the man's hand. Her body reacted before her mind fully processed the threat. Time grinned to a halt, the sounds of the surroundings dissipated until all she could focus on was the gun, its muzzle aimed directly at Cameron and Kirk. She screamed at the top of her lungs, her voice cutting through the solemn atmosphere like a blade.

Her heart pounded as she sprinted out of the crowd gathered at the cemetery. She was running so fast she could barely breathe, her lungs burning as she gasped for air. All she could think of was, not again. I can't lose him too. The memory of her mother's lifeless body flashed before her eyes, fueling her frantic dash. Her scream broke through the heavy silence.

"Cameron! Kirk!" she shrieked, her voice raw with terror. Her finger pointed toward the approaching threat.

Cameron and Kirk spun around, the gravity of the situation hitting them immediately. Without hesitation, both men dove to the ground, narrowly avoiding the bullets that ripped through the air.

Diamond dropped to her knees; her hands clasped tightly in prayer. "Please, God," she begged through her tears, her voice trembling. "Not like this. Not Cameron. Don't take him away from me like you took my mother."

From a distance, Blair, standing with Kennedy and Skee turned in alarm. Skee had been distracted, stepping away to take a phone call, and didn't immediately register the chaos. But Blair did. She caught sight of one of the other shooters just as his weapon began to rise, his black baseball cap pulled low over his eyes.

By this time, Kennedy was crouched behind a near-by stone, her eyes darting frantically, searching for the source of the commotion, dialing her phone with shaking fingers. "We need help now," she hissed into the line as she peered around the corner, trying to locate the shooters.

"Diamond!" Blair screamed, racing toward her friend without hesitation. As she ran, time seemed to slow. The panicked mourners screamed and the sound of feet scattering, seeking cover behind tombstones and trees as chaos spread through the cemetery.

She scrambled toward Diamond, grabbing her arm and yanking her down to the ground just as a bullet grazed the air where Diamond had been kneeling moments before. Both women hit the grass, breathing hard as they clung to each other for safety.

"Stay down!" Blair barked, her heart pounding.

Diamond looked at her with wide, tear-filled eyes. "Thank you," she whispered, her voice barely audible above the commotion.

Faint sirens began to wail, but they seemed too far away to be of immediate help.

Kirk noticed Blair's movement. His eyes darted from Blair to one of the shooters, who had shifted his aim toward her. Without thinking, Kirk broke into a sprint, his long strides closing the distance between them.

The gunman fired. The crack of the shot tore through the air as Kirk reached Blair, tackling her to the ground and shielding her with his body. The bullet struck a nearby tombstone, sending shards of stone scattering. Blair gasped, her chest heaving as she realized how close she had come.

"Kirk..." she whispered, her voice choked with emotion. He was still on top of her, his arms braced to protect her from further harm.

"You, okay?" he asked, his voice calm despite the chaos around them.

Blair nodded, tears streaming down her face.

As the sound of sirens began to grow louder, signaling the approaching police, the shooters retreated, their mission incomplete.

Cameron came running towards Diamond, who was still down on the ground. "We gotta get out of here! Now!" he said, his voice firm. He wrapped his arms protectively around Diamond, helping her to her feet, while Kirk helped Blair, his hand lingering on her arm.

Blair's gaze lingered on Kirk, a realization dawning in her mind. She had been ready to leave for Los Angeles with Skee, to chase her dreams of being an A-List actress, but in this moment, everything shifted. Kirk had risked his life to protect her, to ensure she could return home to their son, even in the midst of their custody battle. She couldn't ignore that.

As Skee approached, his expression a mix of confusion and concern, Blair turned to him. Skee opened his mouth to say something, but the look in Blair's eyes told him all he needed to know.

"We have to go!" Cameron shouted with urgency, uncertain if more gunfire would erupt. They all scurried across the cemetery, staying low and hoping they would reach safety before the next barrage of bullets flew their way.

The gunfire ceased, replaced by police sirens. Diamond's world narrowed to a pinpoint, focused solely on holding onto Cameron in the aftermath.

Suddenly, the scene shifted. The acrid smell of gunpowder gave way to the rich aroma of freshly brewed coffee and warm pastries. Diamond blinked, disoriented by the abrupt transition from past memory to current reality.

"Earth to Diamond," Kennedy's voice cut through her trance. "Where'd you go just now?"

Diamond shook her head, forcing a smile as she took in her surroundings. The upscale New York restaurant bustled with the Sunday brunch crowd. Sunlight streamed through floor-to-ceiling windows, glinting off polished silverware and crystal glasses.

"Sorry," Diamond murmured, reaching for her mimosa. "Just got lost in thought for a second."

Blair leaned in, concern etching her delicate features. "You okay, babe? You looked like you were a million miles away."

Diamond nodded, her fingers absently tracing the rim of her glass. "Yeah, I'm good. Just... remembering things I'd rather forget, you know?"

"I definitely know what you mean," Blair nodded, her mind now seeming to drift off.

"I know this is random, but sometimes, I still wake up in the middle of the night to the sound of gunshots echoing in my head," Diamond sighed. "My mother lost her life to gun violence, and even her funeral was disrupted by the same brutality."

Kennedy reached across the table, squeezing Diamond's hand. "I know how painful that still has to be for you. But we're here now, together. That's what matters."

"I can't lie, I think about the shooting all the time too. I would be dead if it wasn't for Kirk. I'm still traumatized about that day," Blair admitted.

"I would never minimize what happened, but try to focus on the positives," Kennedy said gently. "Diamond, you leaned on Cameron to get through the tragedy, and that saved your marriage. And Blair," she turned to her, "Kirk saving your life made you realize he was the man for you—not Skee."

"True," Diamond and Blair said simultaneously. It was as if on cue, a waiter approached with a tray of colorful appetizers. "Ladies, your lobster avocado toast and truffle fries."

The familiar routine of sharing food and conversation gradually eased the women back into the present. Diamond took a deep breath, inhaling the comforting scents of friendship and normalcy, determined to leave the ghosts of the past behind—at least for now. She sat down her mimosa, her eyes sparkling with newfound determination. "Ladies, I've been thinking. It's time we take control of our narrative; you know? I want to launch a women's empowerment brand."

Blair and Kennedy exchanged intrigued glances as Diamond continued, "I'm talking about a platform that celebrates our strength, our resilience. Something that speaks to women who've been through hell and came out swinging."

She gestured emphatically, her delicate pear and marquise-shaped diamond bangle bracelets jingling. "Imagine workshops, podcasts, maybe even a clothing line. All focused on building each other up, sharing our stories."

Kennedy nodded slowly, considering. "That's... actually brilliant, Diamond. You've always had a talent for motivating others. Remember when you were shot by Lela and became paralyzed? The doctors said you would never walk again, but you defied their expectations and triumphed over the odds."

Diamond's smile was gentle as she reflected on that time in her life and the tremendous dedication she invested in regaining her ability to walk.

"I'm in," Blair said, grinning. "Whatever you need, girl. This could be huge."

Diamond felt a surge of excitement. "I knew you'd get it. We've been through so much, and it's time to turn that pain into power."

Blair clapped her hands together, her enthusiasm infectious. "Speaking of power moves, well," she put her hand up and took a deliberate pause. "It's not a blockbuster movie with me as the leading lady, but after being completely out of the industry loop, guess who just booked a major cosmetic campaign?"

Diamond and Kennedy leaned in; eyes wide. Blair's smile was radiating as she announced, "That's right, your girl's the new face of Pat McGrath. Full blitz, commercials, magazines, social media platforms, the works. National baby!"

"Blair!" Kennedy squealed, reaching across to hug her friend. "That's amazing!"

"It's about damn time," Diamond added, raising her glass in a toast. "To Blair, finally getting the recognition she deserves."

Blair basked in the moment, her eyes shining. "I'm not sure how I managed to forget. You'd think I would've learned from when I took time off after Donovan was born, that in this industry, once you step away, it's damn near impossible to regain people's attention. But humbling myself finally paid off. After all the small gigs, the rejections... this feels like my big break, you know?"

"Because it is," Diamond affirmed. "You've being working yo' ass for this, so we're right here, cheering you on."

Blair took a sip of her drink, her voice softening. "I couldn't have done it without you two. All those nights I felt like a loser and wanted to give up, and battling with Kirk because he wants me to be a stay-at-home NBA housewife, but you all kept giving me the pep talks."

"That's what we do," Kennedy smiled. "We lift each other up."

"That's right," Diamond cosigned.

"Blair, I have to ask," Kennedy inquired. "You clearly love Kirk, and you all share a son, but unlike Skee, he has never fully supported your ambitions to become a successful actress. Do you ever regret choosing to leave Skee?"

Blair paused, her gaze drifting into the distance as she considered Kennedy's question. Memories of her past love, Skee, intertwined with the complexities of her present life with Kirk, creating a tapestry of emotions she often tried to suppress.

"I don't regret leaving Skee," Blair finally replied, her voice tinged with a hint of wistfulness. "We had our time together, but we were on different paths. Kirk and I... there's a history there, a shared journey that runs deeper than what many see on the surface."

Kennedy nodded, her eyes reflecting understanding. "But does his lack of support for your acting career ever weigh on you? Do you feel torn between your love for him and your desire to chase your dreams?"

Blair exhaled softly, the breath carrying a blend of resignation and determination. "Yes, of course I feel torn at times. It is difficult, but I refuse to let it break me. I want it all and I'll make it happen."

As their brunch continued, the energy at the table was full of optimism and possibilities. Diamond could feel it—a shift in the air, a sense that they're on the cusp of something extraordinary. Together, they would not just be surviving; they'd be ready to thrive.

However, Kennedy's smile began to fade slightly as she swirled the ice in her mimosa. "I wish I had you all's optimism," she said, her voice tinged with worry. "I thought by now, I would've figured out a way to get my company back from Darcy, but it's been a struggle. I'm starting to feel that Glitz Inc. will never be mine again."

Diamond and Blair exchanged concerned glances. "What happened, Kennedy? I thought you found dirt on Darcy to reclaim your company." Diamond asked, putting her napkin down.

Kennedy sighed, her shoulders slumping in defeat. "Lyric's intel wasn't as reliable as she claimed. I suppose it's my fault for putting my faith in a woman who filmed her own sex video with a married man and broadcasted it to the world to gain fame."

"Raggedy bitch," Diamond muttered.

"I'm sorry." Kennedy said. "That was tactless of me, considering that married man was your husband."

"No need to apologize. Lyric and Cameron are the ones to blame for the misery that leaked video caused me. You have every right to vent. We're your best friends, that's what we are here for," Diamond reassured her.

Kennedy nodded; her expression grateful for Diamond's understanding. "I just can't believe I let myself get played by Darcy. I feel like I'm losing my touch." She ran a hand through her sleek bob, a telltale sign of her distress.

Blair reached across the table, her eyes glinting with defiance. "Don't give up now. There has to be a way to expose her, to reclaim what's rightfully yours."

Diamond placed a hand on Kennedy's shoulder, offering a reassuring squeeze. "We're in this together. We'll brainstorm, strategize, and come up with a plan that Darcy won't see coming."

Kennedy's eyes flickered with unspoken emotions. "I appreciate that, but what if we can't?" she lowered her voice, vulnerability etched in every word. "I'm scared, y'all. That agency is everything to me."

"We've all endured our fair share of obstacles," Blair's voice was soft but steady. She knew that each of them carried their own burdens, their own battles fought behind closed doors. "But it's how we rise from the ashes that truly defines us."

"Exactly. We've been through worse and come out stronger!" Diamond gave a triumphant fist pump. "We'll figure this out, one way or another. Together."

Kennedy felt a renewed sense of purpose blossoming within her and a surge of gratitude for the friendships that had sustained her through the highs and lows of life. In that moment, she leaned into the warmth of friendship, finding solace in the knowledge that no matter how turbulent her journey became, she had a fierce tribe of women by her side, ready to lift her up

The three women shared a moment of silence, the bond between them almost tangible. They'd weathered storms together, celebrated victories, and now, facing new challenges, their unity was unwavering.

Blair raised her glass. "To us. To overcoming whatever life throws our way."

"To us," Diamond and Kennedy echoed.

As their glasses clinked together, a tall, impeccably dressed waiter approached their table. His crisp white shirt and black vest exuded an air of elegance that matched the upscale restaurant's ambiance. The women's laughter faded as they noticed his slightly furrowed brow and the small, cream-colored envelope nestled on his silver tray.

"Excuse me, ladies," he said, his voice low and professional. "This was left at the host station for your table. The sender insisted it be delivered immediately."

Diamond's eyes widened, a glimmer of unease crossing her face. She reached for the envelope, the texture of thick paper between her fingers. Blair leaned in, her curiosity piqued, while Kennedy's brow creased, sensing the unusual nature of this interruption.

"Thank you," Diamond murmured, dismissing the waiter with a nod.

As the waiter retreated, the women huddled closer, their mimosas momentarily forgotten. A delicate scent, reminiscent of aged parchment and secrecy, wafted from the unsealed flap as Diamond carefully opened the envelope.

"Who would be sending us a note here?" Blair whispered, her voice marked with both curiosity and apprehension.

Kennedy watched closely, the muscles in her neck tensing. "I don't know, but it feels... deliberate."

Diamond unfolded the note. The message was concise, the handwriting a meticulous scrawl that none of them recognized:

"Be careful. The past isn't done with you yet."

A heavy pause hung in the air, dense and charged like the atmosphere before a storm. Their expressions shifted from confusion to concern as they absorbed the ominous words.

"Is this some kind of sick joke?" Blair asked, her voice betraying a hint of fear she tried to mask with bravado.

"Does it look like I'm laughing?" Diamond retorted, her heart pounding against her ribcage. She searched her friends' faces for answers they didn't have. "You think this is about—"

"Shh," Kennedy cut in, glancing around the room to ensure no ears were intruding. "We can't talk about this here."

"Right," Blair agreed, straightening in her seat. "But we need to figure out what this means. And fast."

"Could be nothing," Diamond shrugged, though her facial expression betrayed her true thoughts. "But then again, we've made plenty of enemies through our careers, significant others or both."

"Let's not jump to conclusions," Kennedy advised, always the level-headed one. "We'll meet up later, somewhere private, and discuss our next move."

"Agreed." Blair nodded, her eyes scanning the crowd for potential threats or familiar foes.

"Okay," Diamond said, slipping the note back into its

envelope. Her mind raced with possibilities, each more unsettling than the last.

"Focus ladies," Kennedy added. "Whatever this is, we face it together. Like always."

"Like always," Diamond and Blair echoed, their unity solidified by the unknown threat lurking within the neatly penned warning.

Kennedy reached across the table, her touch firm on Diamond's wrist. "We've overcome worse," she said, her gaze unwavering. "Remember that."

Blair exhaled, her eyes flickered to the window, where the sun cast glimmers of light on the New York skyline, a stark contrast to the darkness creeping into their conversation.

"Let's not spiral here," Diamond urged, her tone steady despite the palpable unease. "We're in control. We'll handle this like we handle everything else—in our own way."

Their meals lay untouched, a tableau of luxury ignored for the moment. The waiter passed by with a questioning glance, but they waved him off, their focus inward on the turmoil the note had stirred.

The three women exchanged looks that held years of shared trials and triumphs. They'd risen together, a trinity against the turbulence of life's unpredictability, and this piece of paper was merely another test—one they would face head-on.

As they stood, the restaurant's ambiance enveloped them again—the laughter, the clinking glasses, the scent of gourmet cuisine. However, every step they took was deliberate, their senses sharpened by the ominous feeling that now tinged every glance and movement.

They parted ways at the entrance, sunlight casting long shadows on the pavement. Their silhouettes projected the image of unshakable confidence, but the chill that ran down their spines spoke of the storm that might be brewing just beyond the horizon.

Chapter Two

Blair's Spotlight Reclaimed

The moment Blair's stiletto heels clicked against the polished concrete floor of the Pat McGrath campaign set; a surge of adrenaline coursed through her veins. Her gaze flitted across the pulsating hive of activity — stylists fluttering around like eclectic birds of paradise, photographers checking their lenses with the scrupulous attention of surgeons, and assistants zigzagging with an urgency that was almost palpable.

"Showtime," she murmured to herself, the words barely audible over the cacophony of creative chaos.

With a deep breath that swelled her chest beneath the silk blouse, she stepped further into the fray, her heart performing an erratic dance of excitement and trepidation. This was more than just another photoshoot; it was the resurrection of her career, the potential phoenix-rising moment she had replayed in her mind during those silent nights when doubt was her only companion.

"Blair!" A voice cut through the pandemonium, smooth and welcoming. It was Marco, the lead makeup artist, his arms open as if ready to catch her should the gravity of the moment pull her down.

"Darling, you look ravishing," he cooed, his fingers already reaching for her face with the delicacy of a maestro poised to compose a masterpiece.

"Thank you, Marco." Blair's response was a cocktail of humility and practiced grace, the warmth of her smile never reaching the nervous flutter in her stomach. She settled into the makeup chair, allowing the transformative power of brushes and pigments to sweep away any lingering unease.

"Ready to shine?" Marco asked, his eyes meeting hers in the mirror.

"Always," she replied, the word a vow to herself as much as it was an answer to him.

Once primed and prepped, Blair emerged like a vision onto the set proper, the camera beckoning her with its unblinking eye. The photographer, Nina, greeted her with a nod, her expression an intriguing blend of artistic hunger and professional respect.

"Let's make magic," Nina said, her voice threaded with anticipation.

Blair took her position, feeling the heat of the lights

as a physical weight upon her skin. Yet, within this cruci-ble, she found her strength. With every snap of the shut-ter, she moved, her body flowing from one pose to the next with an elegance that belied the internal tremor she fought to control.

"Perfect, Blair! Hold that," Nina directed, her tone sharpening with excitement.

"Like this?" Blair arched an eyebrow, her lips curv-ing in a playful challenge that matched the daring glint in her eye. She wore a simple dress so as not to detract from the flawless beauty of her face and makeup. The soft, smooth fabric draped elegantly over her curves, with a slight sheen that caught the lights and gave her a glamor-ous sheath with the deep turquoise color complementing the warmth of her skin, with bold dark eyes and a subtle pink lip. The neckline was modest yet flattering, and the silhouette flowed gracefully around her body.

"Exactly like that," Nina confirmed, capturing the image with a satisfied click.

Between flashes, Blair connected with the crew, her laughter genuine, her comments insightful. Each mem-ber became a thread in the tapestry of her performance, and she wove them together with the careful skill of a weaver at her loom. The essence of the campaign — bold, unapologetic beauty — was not just depicted in the im-ages they created; it was embodied by Blair herself.

And as the camera continued to capture the myr-iad facets of her persona, something inside Blair began to solidify. This was no mere return; it was a declaration that Blair Dupont, the woman who had once watched her dreams slip through her fingers like grains of sand, was back with the might of a tempest, ready to reclaim what was hers. The frenetic energy of the set ebbed momentarily as Blair stepped away, a brief intermission in the day's symphony of creativity. Her fingers wrapped around the cool surface of a water bottle, condensation dampening her skin as she took a long, steadying sip. She leaned against a vacant stretch of wall, a silent observer to the hive of activity before her.

On the monitors, a cascade of images flickered past — each frame a testament to her resurgence. The sharp angles of her cheekbones, the commanding tilt of her chin, the fire in her gaze; every detail was an affirmation of her presence, a siren call to those who witnessed it. There was a raw honesty in those photographs, a narrative woven without words that spoke of resilience, of beauty rising from the ashes of doubt and fear.

Blair could feel the pull of the spotlight's warm embrace, its glow reigniting embers she thought had long since cooled. It was intoxicating, this dance with destiny, each measured step leading her further into the light. Yet beneath the heady rush of triumph, there lurked a whisper of trepidation — the knowledge that the higher she soared, the more she risked should she fall.

"Looking good, Blair," a voice called out, pulling her from her thoughts. "We already started posting some of these shots to social media."

"Great and thank you," she replied, her tone steady, though her heart thrummed with the charge of what these images represented. This was more than a campaign; it was a promise to herself, a vow etched in light and shadow. But with the accolades came the weight of expectation, the unspoken demand to outdo not just her peers but also her past self.

With a deep breath, Blair set down her water bottle, rolling her shoulders back as if to shed the mantle of doubt. She would not shy away from this challenge; she would meet it head-on with the grace and tenacity that had brought her to this precipice of change. For now, though, there were more shots to be taken, more moments to capture.

"Let's do this," she murmured, stepping back into the fray, as the incessant buzzing of her phone pulled Blair from the cocoon of her creative bubble. It lay there on the makeup counter, a sleek precursor of the world beyond the studio lights. With each vibration, it beckoned her back to reality.

She picked up the device, thumbing through notifications that cascaded down the screen like a digital waterfall. Comments, likes, shares – each one a tiny affirmation of her relevance, her impact, her return. She felt the swell of pride in her chest, like a balloon inflating with every new mention. But within that same space, another sensation curled tighter – a knot of anxiety. The public eye was fickle, and today's adoration could so easily become tomorrow's scrutiny.

"Blair! You're trending!" one of the assistants squealed, peering over her shoulder with wide-eyed excitement.

"Am I?" Blair responded; her smile genuine but edged with an awareness that fame was as much a storm to weather as it was a sun to bask in. She scrolled past praise and into the predictions, the expectations, the demands. It was all happening so fast; the world seemed ready to propel her forward without asking if she was ready to leap.

As she pondered the dizzying array of emotions, her phone interrupted with a call that demanded her attention. The familiar name of her agent at Elite Talent Agency splashed across the screen

"Hey Gerad!" Blair answered, her voice a blend of anticipation and caution.

"Blair, darling! Have you seen the buzz on social media? It's incredible!" Her agent's voice crackled with electric enthusiasm. "You see what happens when timing and the right campaign perfectly align. Just like that, offers are pouring in. They want you, Blair. They all want you."

A surge of elation coursed through her veins, sweet and heady, like champagne bubbles tickling her senses. This was what she had worked for, dreamed of during those long nights where doubt was her only company. Yet, even as her heart danced to the tune of success, her mind cast a shadow of concern across the bright tableau of her future. How would these opportunities shape her life, the delicate balance she strove to maintain between the woman the world saw, being a mother and the woman who longed for simplicity, for love, for a sense of self untethered from the spotlight?

"Wow, that's... that's amazing," Blair managed, her words measured, betraying none of the whirlwind inside her.

"Let's get together tomorrow to go over everything. We shouldn't delay too much in deciding our next step. The opportunity is ripe, and we need to act now!"

"Understood," Blair replied, her gaze drifting to the hive of activity around her, each person oblivious to the crossroads at which she now stood. She ended the call, tucking away the phone as if by doing so she could also stow her burgeoning apprehension.

"Everything okay?" asked a nearby photographer, sensing the subtle shift in her demeanor.

"Better than okay," Blair affirmed, bolstering her resolve with a smile. "Just navigating the next steps."

"Good for you," he said, giving her an encouraging nod. "Ready to go again?"

"Of course, let's make magic," she answered, not just to the crew, but to herself, to the universe, to anyone who might be listening. And with the flash of the camera, Blair once again became the image of confidence, even as she stood at the abyss of change, her future unwritten and beckoning with both promise and peril.

The key slipped into the lock with a soft click, and Blair turned the knob, stepping over the threshold into the quietude of domesticity. A shift in the air—a mixture of warmth and apprehension—greeted her as she closed the door behind her, the sound muffled in the spacious hallway. The penthouse was dimly lit; shadows stretched across the walls as the evening sun began its descent.

"Mommy!" The voice of her son, Donovan, would usually slice through the quiet, but tonight it was Kirk's presence that dominated the space. Because his team didn't make the NBA playoffs, he had nothing but time on his hands. He emerged from the archway leading to the living room, his expression stitched with threads of uncertainty.

"Hey," Blair said, her voice soft, reading the nuances in his tentative smile.

"Hi," Kirk replied, closing the distance between them with a few careful steps. "You're home late."

"Shoot ran over," she explained, setting down her bag, the leather thudding against the hardwood floor.

He nodded, and there was a moment of stillness, a breath held between them before he spoke again. "How did it go?"

"How can I describe it," she began, her eyes lighting up. "The energy on set was—"

"Tense?" Kirk offered the word, one corner of his mouth lifting in a familiar half-smile.

"More like intoxicating, thrilling. I'm finally back!" Blair gushed, reaching out, her fingers brushing against his arm. "But I've missed this, us."

Kirk's gaze held hers, searching, hoping.

"I'm happy for you, Blair. Really, I am. It's just that—"

"Talk to me," she urged gently.

"It's hard to explain." His eyes shifted away for a fraction of a second, betraying a vulnerability he often kept hidden. "With your career taking off again... I don't know where that leaves Donovan and me."

"Kirk, you and Donovan are my world. Nothing changes that." Her words were fervent, sincere.

"I know, I do. But it's like we're on different tracks now, and I'm not sure how to keep up with yours." His shoulders tensed as he confessed, "I'm proud of you, but I also miss you. And I worry how you chasing success will affect our family."

"I'm not chasing success; I'm chasing my dreams. From the very first day we met, my heart's desire was to be a movie star. Just a couple years back, I was on the cusp of that and then..." Blair's voice faded away.

"Then what? Go on, say it. You sacrificed everything for Donovan and me. You resent us for not being this movie star you dreamed of?" Kirk challenged.

"No! I hold myself responsible. Why is it that you don't have to choose between being a basketball player, a father, and a partner to me? Just like you have it all, I want the same," Blair shot back.

"I'm not chasing a dream. I'm already a superstar in the NBA. Everything I do improves the quality of life for you and our son. You're trying to establish a career, while I already have one. You should be planning our wedding. Is pursuing acting gigs worth the time away from your family?" Kirk questioned.

Blair felt the weight of Kirk's words like a physical blow, each syllable a sharp edge slicing through the delicate fabric of their relationship.

"This isn't just about acting gigs, Kirk. This is about reclaiming a part of myself that got lost in the shuffle of motherhood and constantly making myself available to you," Blair spoke, her voice laced with a raw vulnerability. "I love being Donovan's mom, your partner, but I also need to be Blair, the woman who has dreams and ambitions beyond our family unit."

Kirk's expression softened at her words. "I don't wanna be the one holding you back from your dreams. But it's just... hard. Donovan misses you when you're away for long hours. He asks for you at bedtime, and I miss you too."

Blair's heart clenched at the mention of their son longing for her presence. Guilt threaded through her like a poison she couldn't shake off. "Kirk, I always miss both of you when I'm away. But I can't ignore this fire inside me, the passion that drives me to chase after what I've always wanted. I want to be the best mother, partner, and actress I can be. I want Donovan to see me as a woman who didn't let go of her dreams for anyone or anything."

The lines of tension eased from Kirk's face as he listened to her words. "I know you have a passion for this, Blair. I've seen it in your eyes every time you talk about your work. I want you to succeed, to shine like the diamond you are." He reached out to touch her cheek, his thumb brushing away an unshed tear. "I just... I don't want to lose us in the process."

Blair leaned into his touch, feeling the warmth of his hand against her skin. "We won't lose us, Kirk. We'll find a new balance, a way to support each other's dreams while cherishing what we share together."

"I believe in us, and I'll be there for you," Kirk vowed, as he pulled her into a gentle embrace.

Chapter Three

Diamond's Bold Pivot

Diamond confidently strode through the glass doors of the co-working space, immediately enveloped by the buzz of ambition and productivity. She absorbed the sounds of clacking keyboards and animated conversations. The sleek, open-concept design pulsed with energy, each individual absorbed in their own bubble of innovation and drive.

She inhaled deeply, trying to center herself amidst the whirlwind of thoughts that swirled around her head. 'Shine Like a Diamond,' her emerging lifestyle brand, shimmered in her mind's eye—a beacon of potential and empowerment for women everywhere. Yet, beneath this vision of success were the tenuous threads of doubt about her marriage to Cameron, which threatened to unravel her concentration.

"Focus," she whispered to herself, her breath fogging up momentarily on the cool metal of the door handle. She let go of the misted-over metal and straightened her back. Today was about her future, about the seeds of change she was sowing with every choice she made.

Finding her reserved spot, Diamond sank into the ergonomic chair at a sleek, modern workspace that seemed designed for people exactly like her—ambitious, driven, and on the verge of something great. From her leather tote bag, she extracted a notebook, its cover embossed with a diamond pattern that caught the light as if winking at her silently.

This notebook was her sanctuary, a tangible collection of her dreams and ideas. Her fingers traced over the pages reverently, each sketch and scribbled note a breadcrumb on the path back to herself—to the Diamond who didn't second-guess her instincts or shrink her ambitions to fit someone else's mold. Here lay the blueprint of 'Shine Like a Diamond,' not just a brand but a movement, each design a commitment to the journey of reclaiming her independence and identity.

The humiliating cheating scandal with Cameron made Diamond understand that even if she chose to forgive her husband and work on their marriage, she needed to carve out her own path in life, distinct from him. This was essential for maintaining her dignity and protecting her self-esteem from being eroded by his actions. She could still support Cameron while prioritizing self-love.

In the quiet sanctuary of her mind, Diamond could almost hear the voice of her brand speaking to the hearts of women everywhere, telling them they were seen, they were powerful, and they too could shine. It was a message etched into her very soul, and with every breath, she poured it onto these pages. This was her renaissance, her awakening—it was the rebirth of Diamond.

Diamond's concentration on the notebook was punctuated by the clinking of coffee cups and the low hum of conversation when a shadow fell across her sketches. She looked up, and her breath caught—a ghost from her past made flesh. Marcus stood before her there, his presence like a beacon in the busy co-working space. His smile was warm, familiar—a remnant of easier days, and it spread across his face with genuine delight.

"Is this seat taken?" Marcus asked, gesturing to the chair opposite her.

For a moment, Diamond was a teenager again, caught in the charged silence of a high school hallway. But she wasn't that girl anymore; she was a woman who had been through the storm several times. Still, her heart skipped a beat, "Only by ghosts," she laughed as she motioned for him to sit.

"Looks like you're conjuring up some magic here," he observed, nodding at her notebook.

"Only the best kind," Diamond quipped, putting the notebook down and leaning back, allowing herself to take in the full measure of Marcus. He carried himself with an ease that spoke of success and self-assuredness—the stark contrast to the boy she once knew.

"Remember when we used to dream about taking over the world?" Marcus said, a glint of nostalgia in his eyes.

"You mean, you dreamed of wanting to build empires and all I cared about was getting my hair and nails done," Diamond. cracked. Her laughter was light, unburdened by the weight of her recent troubles.

"I see you're still keeping your hair and nails done," he remarked with a smile, his gaze sweeping over her sketches before settling on her face, "By the looks of it, you're on your way to building something extraordinary."

"Thanks to lessons learned from the past, I suppose," she replied, her thoughts briefly drifting to Cameron, but she shook them away, refocusing on the present.

"It seems that while some things have changed since our past, much remains the same as it was in tenth grade. I've swapped my bifocals for cataract surgery, and you, well, you're still pretty as ever," Marcus mused, with a slight smile.

"Thank you," Diamond said blushing. "You know, I always thought you looked adorable with your glasses."

"Not adorable enough," he chuckled. "You did dump me for that guy who used to pick you up from school in the tricked-out Benz," Marcus reminded her.

"I never apologized for that. I was so dumb back then," Diamond admitted, genuinely remorseful about how she treated her high school sweetheart.

"No apology needed. What was his name again... and how is he doing?"

"Rico, and he's not doing very well. He's dead."

"Oh wow, I'm sorry to hear that."

"Don't be. He was the worst boyfriend ever. Dumping you for him was the biggest mistake of my life," Diamond sighed. "Actually, I take that back because we had a beautiful daughter together," she smiled.

"Nice. What's her name?" Marcus asked.

"Destiny."

"Is she your only child?"

"No, I also have a son Elijah."

"And I'm guessing that's who you're married to," Marcus nodded, glancing at the ring on her finger.

"Yes," Diamond twisted the diamond ring on her finger absently. "We share a son together and he is also a father to Destiny."

"That's beautiful. I'm glad to see you thriving, Diamond," Marcus said sincerely. "You've always had a spark in you that was meant to shine bright."

The compliment, simple and sincere, wrapped around Diamond like a blanket of validation. She felt a sense of gratitude for the unexpected reunion with Marcus. There was this sense that perhaps this encounter was more than just coincidence. Here was someone who knew her before life added its layers of complexity. Someone who still saw her, not just the wife of a man embroiled in scandal, but Diamond—bright, fierce, unyielding.

"Thank you, Marcus. That means more than you know," she said, her voice warm, their shared history amplifying the weight of his words. "Marriage can be challenging especially when you're married to an NBA player. Things have been complicated," she admitted.

"NBA player...do I know who he is?"

"Cameron Robinson."

"Definitely know that name," Marcus nodded

"I won't pry, but I'm here if you ever need to talk," Marcus offered, his expression one of genuine concern.

The sincerity in his offer touched Diamond in a way she hadn't expected. In that bustling co-working space, amidst the clatter and buzz of ambition and dreams being chased, a bond from the past rekindled, offering a glimpse into a future where Diamond might shine even brighter—with or without Cameron. The encounter with Marcus was a reminder that her story wasn't written yet, and chapters full of hope and healing lay ahead, waiting to be penned by her own hand.

Diamond leaned forward, elbows resting on the sleek tabletop, as Marcus launched into his latest triumphs in the tech world. He spoke with animated gestures, a dance of hands painting pictures of innovation and success.

"Last quarter, we rolled out this augmented reality platform that's revolutionizing the shopping experience," Marcus said, his eyes alight with passion. "It's like bringing the store to your living room, making everything more personal, more real."

Diamond listened, mesmerized by the way Marcus's achievements seemed to unfold before her like a road map of what could be. Each sentence he spoke was drenched in the excitement of possibility, and she felt herself drawn into the gravity of his world—a world where ideas sparked and caught fire, burning bright against the skyline of progress.

"Your ambition is incredible, Marcus," Diamond praised, feeling a surge of inspiration. "It's amazing to think I knew you when we used to gaze at the sky, and you'd share all your dreams with me."

"We all have our paths, Diamond. And speaking of dreams, tell me more about what you're working on?"

Diamond unfolded her notebook, revealing the sketches and concepts that were the lifeblood of her brand. "It's called Shine Like a Diamond. All about empowering women—through fashion, through message, through community."

"Empowerment... I love that," Marcus nodded, moving closer. His gaze lingered on her designs, genuine interest lighting up his features. "You know," he began thoughtfully, "I could help you with that. The digital space is prime real estate for a brand like yours."

Diamond blinked, taken aback by the offer. "You'd do that? Help me?"

"Of course," Marcus said earnestly. "Consider it my contribution to making sure your light shines as brightly as possible."

A laugh, pure and unguarded, escaped Diamond's lips. A renewed sense of hope unfurled within her chest, warming her like the glow of a sunrise after a long, stormy night. Here was an opportunity, unexpected and thrilling, that could catapult 'Shine Like a Diamond' into the hearts and lives of women everywhere.

"Thank you, Marcus," she said, her voice thick with emotion. "This could change everything."

"Then let's make it happen, Diamond. Let's make sure the whole world sees you shine."

As they delved into potential strategies, Diamond's heart swelled. The prospect of her brand reaching new heights intertwined with the serendipitous reconnection to a past love, creating a whirlwind of excitement and potential. She was ready to embrace this chapter.

That evening, Diamond's mind lingered on Marcus and their ambitions for Shine Like a Diamond. So absorbed was she in her reflections that she nearly missed her phone buzzing with a message from Cameron. She glanced at it, sensing the usual inner turmoil, but this time, she placed the phone back down without a second thought. There would be moments later to ponder matters of love and fidelity, but not now. She wanted to relish the excitement of this new chapter in her life.

"Chase the dreams that scare you," she murmured, a mantra that pulsed with the beat of her heart. There was power in admitting to the dreams that loomed large and daunting, the ones that promised both fulfillment and the peril of disappointment. Yet, in acknowledging them, she also acknowledged her capacity to rise and meet their demands.

She envisioned her brand reaching women across the globe, an inspiration for professional growth, personal empowerment merged into one brilliant trajectory. With the support and acumen of Marcus, Diamond had no doubt her dreams would come true.

Chapter Four

Kennedy's Crisis

Kennedy sat at her sleek desk, fingers hovering over the keyboard of her laptop, her mind tangled in knots. The city skyline twinkled outside the towering windows of the high-powered PR agency where she still worked as a senior account executive. Despite her success here, her mind was consumed with one thing—getting Glitz Inc. back from Darcy and Michael. Every strategy she had devised thus far had fallen short, and Lyric Nunez, was proving to be a dead end. The dim glow from the monitor illuminated the determined set of her jaw. The office was nearly empty—most of her colleagues had long since gone home—but she remained, drowning in work and an insatiable need for sweet revenge.

She had spent an absorbent amount of time prying into Lyric Nunez's past dealings with Darcy and Michael, hoping the reality star held the ammunition she needed to reclaim Glitz Inc. But every conversation, every strategically placed question, had led to a dead end. Lyric had no incriminating secrets, no hidden scandals that could be wielded against her nemesis. It was maddening.

A soft knock at her office door startled her. She turned to see Sebastian standing in the doorway, holding a brown paper bag and a knowing smile.

"I figured you'd still be here. You look like you could use a break. Thought I'd surprise you," he said, stepping inside and placing the bag on her desk. "You forget to eat when you're plotting world domination."

Kennedy let out a small, tired laugh. "More like trying to take back what's mine."

Sebastian took a seat across from her, watching as she reached into the bag and pulled out a container of pasta. The smell of garlic and basil filled the room, momentarily breaking the tension that had settled into her bones.

"I take it things with Lyric are still not panning out?" Sebastian asked, his sharp gaze studying her.

Kennedy sighed, twirling the pen in her fingers before setting it down. "She's got nothing on them. No scandals, no backroom deals, nothing that I can use." She looked up at him, frustration flickering in her eyes. "I thought if I could just find one piece of dirt, I could take them down and get my company back."

Sebastian leaned back in his chair, crossing his arms. "And if you did find something? Then what?"

"I would take those fucks down and reclaim my

company," she snapped as if Sebastian had posed a ridiculous question.

Sebastian studied her for a long moment before speaking. "I get it, Kennedy. I do. They stole your dream. But you need to be careful. You start playing their game, digging for dirt, crossing ethical lines—it's a slippery slope."

She exhaled sharply, pushing the pasta container away as she leaned back in her chair. "So what? I just let them win?"

"No," he said firmly. "But you don't let them turn you into them either."

Kennedy looked away, her mind warring between the desperate need to take Darcy and Michael down and the wisdom in Sebastian's words.

Sebastian reached across the desk, gently placing his hand over hers. "You built Glitz from the ground up once. You can do it again. But you need to be smart about it. Don't let revenge consume you."

Kennedy swallowed hard. She wasn't sure she was ready to let go of her anger, but for the first time since the battle began, she allowed herself to consider a different path. Maybe there was another way to win. Kennedy's eyes hardened.

"I already lost everything once. I won't let it happen again."

Sebastian sighed, realizing he wouldn't change her mind. "Just... promise me you won't do something reckless."

"I promise to do whatever it takes," Kennedy countered.

As Sebastian left, Kennedy turned back to her screen, her mind spinning. If Lyric couldn't help, she'd find another way. Darcy and Michael had taken everything from her, and she wasn't about to let them get away with it.

As the city lights continued to dance outside her window, casting a surreal glow over her determined face, Kennedy's mind raced with a storm of strategies, each one more aggressive than the last. There was only one objective, which tactic would deliver the most powerful result. She knew she had to tread carefully, but the fire of vengeance burned bright within her.

The next morning, Kennedy arrived at the office earlier than usual. The building was still waking up as she settled at her desk, a steaming cup of coffee in hand. Purpose glittered in her eyes as she opened a new document on her laptop, fingers flying over the keyboard.

She began crafting a bold plan, one that didn't rely on finding scandalous secrets or dirty tactics. It would require patience, finesse, and a touch of cunning. Kennedy was going to outmaneuver Darcy and Michael at their own game, but she wouldn't sacrifice her integrity in the process.

Throughout the day, Kennedy worked tirelessly, reaching out to old contacts, forging new alliances, and laying the groundwork for her daring scheme. Colleagues glanced curiously sensing a shift in her energy, a new fire burning beneath her posh and steely exterior. Kennedy was no longer just a senior account executive—she was a force to be reckoned with, a woman on a mission.

As the day turned into night once again, Kennedy found herself poring over stacks of documents, her phone buzzing intermittently with messages from sources she had reached out to. The pieces of her plan were falling into place, each one a steppingstone towards her ultimate goal.

Just as she was about to call it a night and head home, her phone buzzed with an incoming call. It was Lyric.

"What can I do for you Lyric?" Kennedy's voice was dry. Now that she had proven to be of no use to her, Kennedy wasn't motivated to shower Lyric with fake adoration or pretend to be her biggest cheerleader.

"Are you still at the office? I wanted to discuss something with you."

"Yes, but I was about to head out. Can it wait until tomorrow?" Kennedy replied, sounding dismissive.

"It can't wait. I need to talk to you now." Lyric's voice had a pleading tone, which was unusual for her.

"Alright, go on, I'm listening."

"Not over the phone."

Kennedy sighed heavily, clearly annoyed.

"Please, Kennedy."

She felt inclined to refuse, but despite her dislike for Lyric, she was a client who frequently stirred up drama, which was beneficial for business. "I suppose I can wait for you. How long will it take for you to get here?"

"Can we meet for drinks instead?"

"Sure, text me the place. See you soon."

Kennedy tapped the end call button, a mix of curiosity and wariness swirling inside her. Lyric's urgency was unusual, and Kennedy couldn't help but wonder what the reality star wanted to discuss that couldn't wait until the next day.

She quickly gathered her things, slipping her phone into her purse alongside her keys before heading out of the office. The city buzzed around her as she got in her car headed to the address Lyric had sent for their meeting.

The bar was dimly lit, a sultry ambiance that contrasted sharply with Kennedy's mood. She spotted Lyric sitting at a corner table, nervously tapping her 3D gems designed coffin nails on the glass in front of her. She was wearing oversized sunglasses perched on her nose despite the dark interior. Kennedy approached, she noted the tension etched on Lyric's face, a stark departure from her usual overly confident demeanor.

"What's this all about, Lyric?" Kennedy asked sliding into the seat across from her.

"I shouldn't be here," Lyric whispered, her hands nervously fidgeting with a cocktail napkin.

Kennedy arched a brow. "You called me, remember?"

Lyric exhaled sharply, glancing around before leaning in. "I need your help, Kennedy. I—" She hesitated, pressing her lips together before continuing in a hushed tone. "I messed up. Bad. I didn't know who I should trust with this information, but you've always shown me love, so I felt I could come to you."

Kennedy leaned in as well, her curiosity piqued. "Go on."

Lyric swallowed hard. "Back when I was a client of Darcy's, she and Michael... they had me front a fake charity. They said it was a way to reduce my taxes and keep a ton of money in my pockets. They claimed everyone in the industry did it and it was no big deal. That was a lie. It's a major deal. They used that charity to launder money—for themselves, and certain clients. I've ran my fair share of scams in the past, so I figured they were involved in some shady shit. But not on me doing no federal prison time type level. I swear. Once Darcy spilled the true tea, I was already in too deep."

Kennedy's jaw tightened. "And now?"

"The IRS is sniffing around. Journalists too." Lyric's voice trembled. "If this gets out, my career is over. I could go to prison. I need you to help me clean this up."

Kennedy sat back, her mind already spinning through the possibilities. This was it—the leverage she needed against Darcy and Michael. But could she trust Lyric to follow her lead?

A slow smile spread across Kennedy's lips. "You're right, Lyric. You're in deep. But lucky for you, I know exactly how to pull you out—on one condition."

Lyric nodded eagerly. "Anything."

Kennedy's eyes gleamed with renewed optimism. "You tell me everything."

Lyric's eyes widened, her grip on the cocktail napkin tightening. "Everything?"

Kennedy nodded; her expression unwavering. She leaned in closer, her tone firm but calculating. "Start from the beginning. Tell me every dirty detail about their operation, fake charity, every shady deal, and how Darcy and Michael roped you into this. Don't leave anything out."

Lyric took a deep breath, her hands trembling slightly as she prepared to share all the secrets that she had been holding on to. Kennedy watched her intently, her mind already formulating a plan to use this newfound information to her advantage. As Lyric began to recount the intricate web of deceit spun by Darcy and Michael, the contact high she was getting was more addictive than any narcotic you could purchase on the street.

After Lyric finished divulging every devious crime the duo committed, Kennedy leaned back in her seat, a calculating glint in her eyes. "You made the right decision speaking up. Our pr firm has to address this before the media can twist it," she remarked, as if expressing concern for her client. However, Kennedy had grander schemes for the information Lyric had provided, plans that were not meant for Lyric to be privy to.

"You can't let the media discover this! That's why I came to you," Lyric exclaimed, her voice tinged with panic.

"Calm down." Kennedy placed a reassuring hand on Lyric's arm, her touch comforting. "Don't worry, I've got this under control. I have a plan, but you have to trust me on this. Once this is over, you'll simply be another innocent victim, oblivious to the illicit schemes of Darcy and Michael."

Lyric's eyes widened. "Perfect! What do you need me to do?"

"We're going to turn the tables on them. But we need to be strategic and meticulous. Are you ready for this?"

"I'll do whatever it takes." Lyric seemed to relax slightly, her features softening but she was unable to mask her desperation.

"Listen carefully." Kennedy's gaze was sharp, a predator assessing its prey before making the final strike. The information Lyric had shared was like a well-sharpened blade in her hands, ready to strike at the heart of their deceitful empire. She had the ammunition she needed now; and it was time to take down Darcy and Michael once and for all.

Packer sat on the worn-out couch in the prison's common area, his arms crossed as he stared at the television. A rerun episode of Lyric's reality show played on the screen, her signature smirk plastered across her face as she twirled a glass of champagne in her hand, living the glamorous life.

Packer's jaw tightened, rage simmering beneath the surface. "Look at this bitch," he muttered under his breath.

The inmate next to him, a burly guy with a face full of tattoos, glanced at the screen and then back at Packer. "You know her or somethin'?"

Packer let out a bitter chuckle. "Oh, I know her. That's a foul bitch. Fucked a muthafucka I can't stand, that basketball nigga Cameron Robinson. She did that shit while living wit' me, then leaked the fuckin' video to get famous and broke out."

The other inmate smirked. "Damn. Cold but it worked," he nodded glancing back up at the television as Lyric sashayed across the screen.

Packer's eyes darkened. "Yeah, it worked alright. That ain't even the worst part. Before I got locked up, my boys shot up a kid's birthday party tryna take out the nigga she fucked but killed some old lady by mistake."

Tattoo Face whistled low. "Shit, I wouldn't want to be on yo' bad side."

"Nah," Packer said, his voice low and venomous.

"After I finish doing this short stint, I'ma finishing what I started. That bitch Lyric is dead the second I touch the streets."

Tattoo Face nodded approvingly. "Gotta handle business."

Packer leaned forward, staring at Lyric's face on the screen. "She think she safe. Think she won. But she don't even see it comin'."

His lips curled into a sinister grin. "I'm gonna make sure she neva see another fuckin' camera flash again."

Chapter Five

Sisterhood Summit

The golden hue of the setting sunbathed Diamond's penthouse in a warm glow as she opened the door to reveal Blair and Kennedy, standing side by side. With open arms, Diamond welcomed them.

"My two besties, looking stunning as ever!" Diamond's voice resonated with genuine affection as she stepped back, appraising her friends with a smile.

"Girl, this place is always such a vibe," Blair remarked, her gaze sweeping across the spacious room where luxury met comfort in a deliberate dance.

"It really is," Kennedy cosigned.

"Each time I visit, I'm reminded that I should contact the interior designer Kirk recommended to me, so she can help decorate our home. That penthouse still feels too much like a bachelor's pad," Blair grumbled.

"You're a career woman now, it's hard to find the time," Diamond replied, leading them through the grand living area. The plush cream sofas, accented with jewel-toned pillows, beckoned them to sit and shed the weight of the world they carried on their shoulders.

As they settled, the clink of ice against crystal signaled the start of their evening. Diamond filled their glasses with champagne, the effervescence mirroring the excitement that fizzed between them. Yet beneath the surface, a tension hummed—a current of unresolved matters waiting to be discussed.

"Alright, spill it, Blair. You've got that look," Kennedy said, her keen eyes catching the slight furrow in Blair's brow.

Blair sighed, sinking into the cushions, her posture betraying the fatigue she tried to mask with poise. "Since I did that cosmetic campaign, it's been non-stop, you know? Milan was amazing, and the pilot for the new series is looking promising."

"Sounds incredible," Diamond encouraged, her tone both bright and attentive.

"It is, it really is," Blair continued, her hands gesturing expressively as if trying to grasp the whirlwind her life had become. "But Kirk... he's feeling neglected. And I can't blame him. Between shoots and auditions, there's barely a 'we' left in our equation."

"Girl, you're climbing mountains, breaking barriers," Kennedy chimed in, her voice a blend of admiration and concern.

"You were very transparent with Kirk when you decided to once again start pursuing your career. He knows what the deal is," Diamond added, her words laced with conviction. Blair's lips curved into a bittersweet smile, recognizing the truth in Diamond's sentiment.

"To be honest, I don't think Kirk expected me to succeed. During the time I was tirelessly hitting the pavement going from one audition to another and facing constant rejections, he was incredibly supportive, offering me back massages and rubbing my feet. I believe he thought I would eventually quit. However, I persisted, and it finally paid off. Now, Kirk isn't happy that I'm not a failure."

"That figures," Kennedy sneered. "He really shouldn't have underestimated your determination."

"So, what are you going to do?" Diamond questioned.

"I have to find a happy medium. Because I want my family to stay together. The question is, how do I find that balance without losing myself or Kirk? I don't want everything to be a battle with him. Thanks for letting me vent. Who would like to go next?"

"Well, speaking of battles," Kennedy began, her voice cutting through the penthouse's opulence with urgency. "I've got Darcy and Michael right where I want them. The tax fraud evidence is solid. Kissing Lyric's ass for all that time, is finally about to benefit my cause."

"Tax fraud?" Diamond twisted her neck, impressed despite the severity of the situation.

"Yes, and I have the proof," Kennedy said with a tight smile, tapping a nail against the glass tabletop. "They thought they could bury their sins using Glitz Inc. But not on my watch. Although, reclaiming what's mine won't be pretty."

"Nothing worth having ever is," Blair popped, nodding in solidarity. "What has me disgusted is Michael's participation in all this. He's definitely my ex for a reason."

"Which is probably the reason he joined forces with dumbass Darcy in the first place. I bet that piece of shit is bitter you dumped him and thriving without his bullying ass," Diamond smacked.

"We're in agreement with that," Kennedy said, looking at Diamond with approval. "I'm headed back to LA tomorrow and will begin to put in motion my plan to regain Glitz Inc. Michael will regret aligning himself with Darcy to steal my company because of his bruised ego."

"Leaving so soon?" Diamond asked. "You just got to New York."

"Yeah, I wish I could stay longer. I came here for a global creative conference, but my boss needs me to return to LA immediately. It's another reason why I can't wait to be my own CEO again, so I can have more control over my schedule," Kennedy complained.

"Yes, I get it. Nothing like being in control of your own destiny." Diamond strode to the window, the city lights below casting a celestial glow on her features. "Ladies," she began, turning back with a spark igniting her gaze, "it's time I shared something too."

"Spill it, Diamond. You look about ready to burst," Blair teased, breaking the tension with a gentle laugh.

"I'm ready to launch my lifestyle brand," Diamond announced, her hands gesturing as though unveiling an invisible marquee. "I know a few months ago I spoke with you all about Shine Like a Diamond. But my vision has now come to life. It's more than just products. It's empowerment. It's us, women, taking control of our narratives, our dreams."

"Girl, that's incredible!" Kennedy exclaimed; admiration clear in her voice. "You were not playing. Talk about being on your grind!"

"Thank you, but there's more." Diamond paused, vulnerability flickering across her face. "I've reconnected with Marcus," she admitted, the name hanging in the air like a delicate perfume. "It's... complicated."

Blair tilted her head, considering. "Marcus...are you talking about Marcus your high school sweetheart?"

"Yes, that Marcus. He's been a Godsend. He has helped me tremendously, working together to bring my vision to life," Diamond gushed.

"This is unexpected, Marcus being back in your life after all this time. But I haven't seen you this excited in forever, so your collabo must be the right fit," Blair remarked.

"We're both different people now, but yet you're right, we fit perfectly. He completely supports my vision. We're already preparing for the launch party. Letting the industry know Diamond Robinson has arrived."

"I say go for it," Kennedy encouraged, "let the magic happen. I can see Shine Like a Diamond becoming a powerhouse."

"I concur, but don't have too much fun. Remember you're a married woman," Blair added, her tone playful yet edged with caution.

Diamond nodded, absorbing their words. "I'm optimistic and yes I'm very married," she beamed, flashing her massive wedding ring.

As the conversation bounced from business matters

to personal topics, from past heartaches to future aspirations, they shared laughter and insight as if exchanging valuable gems.

"I love that we're all making strides. And Kennedy, you will destroy Darcy and Michael with their tax fraud shit," Blair said confidently, "No one can execute a well thought out plan quite like you."

"Thank you, Blair. Once I regain control of my company, I'd love for you to consider being my main client. And this time, I won't fuck up," Kennedy promised. "No need to answer now, just give it some thought."

"I don't need to think about it. It would be my pleasure," Blair said with a smile. "Besides, I miss having a manager with whom I share both a professional and personal bond. Especially at times like this."

"Times like what...is there something else going on with you?" Diamond asked.

Blair nodded solemnly, choosing to reveal the recent events. She considered the note, ominously folded in her purse. With a sudden shift in energy, she retrieved it, her once playful eyes now darkened with seriousness.

She began unfolding the paper with deliberate fingers. Her voice dropped to a hush as she read aloud, " 'Be careful. Not everyone wants to see you all succeed.'"

The words hung heavy in the air, a stark contrast to moments before. Diamond and Kennedy glanced at each other, then at Blair full of uneasiness. "Where did you get this?" Kennedy questioned.

"It was dropped off with the doorman at our building," Blair said quietly, her usual calm giving way to anxiety. "I asked him who brought it, but he had no clue."

Kennedy's face hardened as she pondered the message. "This could be anyone—from a jealous rival to someone with a vendetta."

"What if it's the same person who left that letter at the restaurant months ago while we were having brunch. Someone from our past?" Diamond questioned, her mind racing through the rolodex of names they had crossed paths with over the years.

"Could be," Blair exhaled, folding the note and placing it back in her bag. "We've all stepped on toes on our way up."

"I've had so much going on with work, I totally forgot about that letter. We hadn't heard anything else from them...until now," Kennedy sighed.

"We'll fight this bullshit together," Diamond declared, her voice steady and sure. "We've never backed down from any challenge thrown our way. This... this is just another test."

"Absolutely," Kennedy agreed, nodding firmly. "Together, we are unstoppable."

"Bad bitches unite," Diamond winked, feeling a surge of strength from her friends' reassurance.

"Always," Blair concluded, as the three of them exchanged determined glances, resolved to uncover the author of the letter.

Diamond's eyes narrowed as she paced the length of her penthouse, the floor-to-ceiling windows casting long shadows that seemed to mirror the growing unease in the room. "Remember that gala last year?" she asked, pausing to glance at Blair and Kennedy. "The one I hosted for NBA wives and girlfriends. You outbid Clarissa during the charity auction. She swore down you did it simply to embarrass her by showcasing Kirk made way more money than her NBA husband. Remember how livid she was and vowed she'd get even."

"I remember that silly shit. Clarissa is all bark, though," Blair countered, her fingers tracing the edge of the warning note as if it might reveal secrets upon contact. "She enjoys being loud and seen too much to leave an anonymous threat."

"Unless she's changing her approach on how to play the game," Diamond mused, her gaze lost in the cityscape below, where the urban night was ablaze with a million lights, each one a story, a victory, or a vendetta.

"We should consider everyone, even those we might dismiss as harmless. It's often the one you least expect," Kennedy asserted. Her mind sifted through past encounters categorizing faces and incidents into potential leads.

"The more I think about it, I believe Diamond is right," Blair said slowly. "It's the same person who delivered that letter to us when we were at brunch?"

"If it is the same person, what the hell is their endgame?" Diamond's question lingered in the air, a palpable tension settling over the trio. As the weight of the unknown threat loomed in the room like an uninvited guest.

Chapter Six

Dilemmas

Blair's heels clicked assertively against the glossy floor as she entered the hive of activity that was the Savage X Fenty Valentine photo shoot. Makeup artists darted like painterly bees, adding bold strokes of color to already striking faces, while photographers adjusted their lenses with the precision of seasoned maestros.

The air crackled with electricity, a blend of musk and hairspray creating an intoxicating cocktail of glamour and anticipation. Blair took a deep breath, the kaleidoscope of sensations grounding her amidst the chaos. She was here, on the precipice of something momentous, her dreams manifesting in real-time as she navigated through racks of luxurious lingerie, passing tables laden with an arsenal of beauty products.

"Places, everyone!" The director's voice cut through the din, and Blair's pulse quickened. As she approached her mark, a deep voice echoed over the bustle, commanding instant silence.

The air inside the studio buzzed with energy as Blair adjusted the straps of her delicate lace lingerie, the bold red fabric accentuating her flawless skin under the bright stage lights. The Savage X Fenty Valentine's shoot was one of the biggest campaigns of her career—a defining moment. But as the cameras flashed and the music pulsed, an unexpected twist sent her heart racing.

"Sorry I'm late, traffic was a beast."

All heads turned toward the entrance where Skee Patron stood. Her ex, his silhouette framed by the studio doorway. He carried himself with the nonchalance of a man who knew his worth and the power he wielded by merely being present. A murmur rippled through the crew; his reputation preceded him, a force in both the music industry and the tabloids.

Blair's breath hitched at the sight of him, every nerve ending buzzing with an awareness that bordered on electric. Memories surged, a tapestry of heated glances, whispered promises, and the sharp sting of goodbyes.

Skee's smile, easy and familiar, bridged the distance as he came closer. It was the same smile that could unravel her composure with its promise of mischief. Whether it was fate or coincidence that brought them together again, there was no denying the spark that still crackled in the air, threatening to ignite old flames.

"Blair," he greeted, his voice smooth as silk, rich with undertones that spoke of their shared history.

"Skee," she replied, her tone even, betraying none of the inner tumult his presence inspired. She was poised, the embodiment of the success she had fought so hard to achieve, yet his arrival stirred the sparks of a past she thought she had left behind.

"Mr. Patron, please follow me; we need to prepare you for the shoot," one of the set assistants said to Skee. He left for a short while and then returned to the set, ready to work.

The superstar rapper, draped in an open silk robe that revealed his chiseled abs, smirked at Blair from across the set. Their eyes locked, and for a suspended heartbeat, the world around them blurred. The unresolved history, the passion, the pain—it all rushed back in an intoxicating wave.

"You still beautiful Blair," Skee murmured as he approached her between shots, his voice a seductive whisper.

Blair swallowed hard, willing herself to stay professional. "I'm here to work, Skee."

"That don't mean we can't talk," he said, a knowing glint in his eyes. "You can't tell me you don't feel it. This... us."

She wanted to deny it. She should have denied it. But the way he looked at her, the way her body reacted—it was dangerous.

Flashes of light punctuated the air, capturing Blair and Skee in a tableau of feigned intimacy. The white backdrop seemed to glow against their silhouettes, every pose a silent conversation laced with the history only they could hear. Their bodies in sync with the rapid shutter clicks. The air between them vibrated with a tension that was as palpable as the bass from the overhead speakers thumping, with Rihanna's sultry voice singing **Wild Thoughts**

I hope you know I'm for the takin'
You know this cookie's for the bakin'
Kitty, kitty, baby, give that thing some rest
'Cause you done beat it like the '68 Jets
Diamonds ain't nothin' when I'm rockin' with you
Diamonds ain't nothin' when I'm shinin' with you
Just keep it white and black as if I'm your sister
I'm too hip to hop around town out here with you

I know I get wild, wild, wild
Wild, wild, wild thoughts
Wild, wild, wild
When I'm with you, all I get is wild thoughts...

Throughout the photoshoot, Blair was reminded of the first time she met Skee. Kennedy had secured her the lead female role in his new music video. After getting glammed up, she stepped onto the set, and Skee didn't even try to conceal how pleased he was with her appearance. She vividly remembered what he said.

"Where in the fuck did you find her?" he stood walking towards Blair. *"You are fuckin' gorgeous. Where have you been...what other video have you done...I can't believe I've never seen you before."*

"Remember when you said I couldn't strike a pose to save my life?" Blair's voice was playful, her gaze fixed on Skee through the camera lens.

"I see you murdering shit now," Skee replied, his grin broadening as he adjusted his stance, complementing her form with his own. Their banter flowed easily, a reminder of closeness that had never quite faded.

"Only thing I'm killin' these days is the game," she quipped back, tossing her hair with a practiced flair.

"Always knew you would," he said, sincerity threading through his teasing tone.

The photographer called for a break, and the set exhaled, the crew retreating to their respective corners. Alone for a moment in the organized chaos, Blair and Skee shared a glance that acknowledged the surrealness of it all.

"Look at you," Skee began, his voice dropping to a more intimate register. "On billboards, magazine covers... I always told you the world wasn't ready for you."

Blair let out a soft laugh, shaking her head in disbelief. "And yet here we are." Blair had to catch herself. Skee had this way of drawing her in, and at the moment, her life with Kirk was going well. She had finally found a sense of balance and didn't want her chemistry with Skee disrupt it.

"I suppose I finally found my path," she mused, her lips curving into a slight pout. There was an edge of wonder, laced with a tinge of melancholy, as they both reminisced about their intense but flawed history together.

"Blair, you know if you ever need—"

"Last Looks!" The director's voice sliced through their moment, and they were once again pulled into the spotlight, leaving the words hanging unfinished, the sentiment understood but unvoiced. Makeup/hair/wardrobe gave one last touchup to Blair and Skee as they returned to their marks, and the shoot resumed. Their shared history folded back into the fabric of the present, threads of past and potential future weaving a complex tapestry neither could unravel just yet.

The static hum of the prison television barely cut through the chatter of inmates in the common area, but Packer's focus was locked on the screen. The bright lights, the glamorous parties, the perfect life Lyric Nunez flaunted on her reality show—it made his blood boil.

"She ain't shit without me," Packer muttered under his breath, jaw tightening as he watched Lyric sip champagne in some extravagant rooftop lounge.

The inmate beside him, the same stocky man covered in tattoos, chuckled. "Still mad about yo' girl playin' you, huh?"

Packer's eyes darkened. "That bitch wouldn't even have no fuckin' reality show if it wasn't for me. She didn't just play me—she used me. Had my name in the dirt while she got famous off my pain."

"Damn," the inmate mused. "What you gonna do when you get out?"

Packer leaned forward, his voice low and full of menace. "She think she safe, livin' that Hollywood life but she got another thing comin'. Soon, I'll be out and all that shit comin' to an end."

His fingers curled into fists. The moment he was out, Lyric was a dead woman walking. Packer's eyes burned with a ferocious determination as he watched Lyric on the screen, her laughter grating on his nerves like nails on a chalkboard. The other inmates in the common area could sense the storm brewing within him, a storm that threatened to unleash chaos once he was back out in them streets.

As the prison television flickered with images of Lyric's lavish lifestyle, Packer's resentment simmered like a pot left unattended on the stove. The contrast between his confined reality and Lyric's world of glitz and opulence fueled his fury, feeding into a desire for retribution that gnawed at his insides.

"You gonna do somethin' crazy, man?" the inmate asked cautiously, a note of caution lacing his tone.

The vein on Packer's forehead pulsed, his eyes unwavering on the screen. "Crazy ain't even close to what she deserves."

There was a dangerous edge to his words, a promise of violence whispered in the stale prison air.

The tattooed inmate shifted uncomfortably, wariness flickering in his eyes. Packer's obsession with revenge was a dark cloud that cast a shadow over even the most casual interactions. He raised an eyebrow, studying the cold determination in Packer's eyes. "Careful, man. You start talking like that, they might add more time to your sentence."

Packer scoffed, waving off the warning. "I ain't scared of no extra time."

The tattooed inmates learned in, his voice barely above a whisper. "You really gonna go after her like that, man?"

Packer couldn't shake the feeling of betrayal that had festered within him since the day Lyric had turned her back on him for fame and fortune. But now, watching her bask in the spotlight, he knew that their story was far from over.

"She needs to pay for what she did to me."

"That Hollywood life ain't nothing to play with. She got connections, man."

A dangerous smile crept onto Packer's lips. "Connections don't mean nothing when you're staring down the barrel of my gun."

The inmate's eyes widened, realization dawning on him that Packer was dead serious.

Chapter Seven

Shine Like A Diamond

Diamond, draped in a shimmering gown that danced with the city's skyline, stood at the entrance of her launch party like the gatekeeper of her own dreams. Her smile was the flash of a camera – bright, inviting, irresistible – as she greeted each guest with a personal touch, a nod, a shared laugh. Her heart, a drum line beneath her couture, pulsed with anticipation for the night ahead.

Diamond navigated through the crowd, an elegant ship amidst waves of admiration and allure. The air throbbed with the energy of the city's elite, women whose influence could turn tides, all drawn here by Diamond's vision.

"Your brand speaks to me, it's like you've given

voice to what we've all been thinking," enthused a fashion mogul, her statement threading through the clamor of the room.

"Thank you," Diamond responded, "It's about lifting each other up, isn't it? About finding power in our unity."

She moved with purpose, this was more than a launch; it was an affirmation of her place among them, a testament to the resilience that had brought her here.

Cinematic in its unfolding, the evening was a montage of connections made, and respect earned, the close-up shots of Diamond's expressive face telling a story of triumph over tribulation, ambition realized through sheer determination and unyielding courage. Each sentence exchanged; a scene stitched into the broader narrative of her life.

The grand ballroom glittered under the warm glow of chandeliers as Diamond stepped onto the stage, her heart swelling with pride. Tonight was her night—the launch of *Shine Like a Diamond*, a celebration of strength, beauty, and resilience. Beside her, Cameron stood, an arm protectively resting around her waist, his hand found the small of her back, a whisper of support without words, and Diamond drew strength from the contact. His presence a silent promise to rebuild their fractured trust. They were two halves of a strained whole, seeking to mend seams stretched by past betrayals. This was their new beginning.

Just as Diamond raised her champagne glass to toast the evening, her radiance of celebration faltered, as the door swung open, admitting a new guest. A hush fell over the crowd. Then a ripple of whispers spread like wildfire. Lyric Nunez had arrived. The very woman who had slept with her husband. The woman whose leaked sex tape had shattered her world. Her eyes locked on the figure clad in crimson—a stark contrast to the soft ambiance of the venue, her silhouette slicing through the optimistic mood like a blade.

Diamond's poised facade cracked for a fleeting second, her heart skipped, the room's chatter fading into a distant echo. Memories surged: whispered accusations, cold silences, and Cameron's betrayed gaze—all remnants of the scandal that had nearly burned their marriage to the ground.

Diamond's grip on her glass tightened, fury bubbling beneath her poised exterior. Her nails dug into her champagne glass, but she forced herself to keep her expression neutral. This was her night, and she wouldn't let Lyric—of all people—steal the spotlight.

Blair and Kirk were standing nearby, and recognizing the rage in her best friend's eyes, she quickly acted. "I'll be back in a moment," she told Kirk, passing him her champagne glass.

"Excuse me," Diamond murmured to Cameron, storming off before he had a chance to stop her. She navigated the crowd, her mind clouded with a tempest of emotions.

Blair, attuned to her friend's shifting tides, caught the storm brewing in Diamond's eyes. She approached Diamond, her face a blend of worry and rapid calculation.

"Hey," Blair whispered, her hand finding Diamond's arm, "Deep breaths, okay? We've got this."

Diamond nodded, drawing in a steadying breath.

"Let's not give her the satisfaction of a scene," Blair continued, her voice a low hum, barely audible over the buzz of conversation. "How about I talk to security? We can have her leave quietly. No drama."

Diamond reflected on Blair's words, noticing the serene tone of her friend's voice, which sharply contrasted with the turmoil raging inside her.

"Alright," Diamond agreed, her voice still edged with an undertone of reluctance.

"I'll handle this," Blair assured her, "Give me one second. Don't crash out. Blend in, smile, and remember—this night is about you and everything you've built." But before Blair could intercept, Lyric sauntered closer, a smirk on her perfectly glossed lips.

"Congratulations, Diamond," she drawled. "I just had to see this for myself."

"You've got some nerve showing up here," Diamond said, her voice steady but cold.

Lyric tilted her head, faux innocence dripping from her tone. "Oh, come on, Diamond. This is a marvelous event. I'm just here to celebrate strong, independent women... like you."

Blair stepped forward; her jaw tight. "You need to leave."

Lyric let out a soft chuckle, taking a slow sip from the flute of champagne she'd somehow acquired. "Relax, Blair. I'm not here to cause a scene. Just wanted to congratulate Diamond on turning her pain into profit. Really inspiring."

That was it. The fury Diamond had been swallowing erupted in a sharp laugh, one that silenced the murmuring crowd. "Pain into profit?" her voice rose, drawing the attention of every guest. "You slept with my husband. And when the sex video leaked, you ran with it. You made a career out of my humiliation!"

Lyric arched an eyebrow, unfazed. "And you're still married to him, aren't you? So, what's the problem?"

"You're the problem," Diamond's tone was becoming more intense. "This is a private event, and you weren't invited, so leave."

Lyric turned, her smile a razor's edge. "Oh, Diamond, darling. Your little soirée needed some real sparkle. I thought I'd oblige."

"Real sparkle?" Diamond's words were ice over steel. "Or did you come to reopen old wounds?"

"Perhaps I simply wanted to see what all the fuss was about," Lyric shot back, her eyes scanning Diamond's poised figure. "After all, everyone loves a comeback story—even if it's more fiction than fact."

The atmosphere was charged with tension, leading the guests around them to speculate whether a ballroom brawl was about to emerge. Diamond's hands clenched at her sides, her nails digging into her palms.

"Your presence here is neither required nor desired," Diamond said, her voice low and controlled. "Leave now!"

"Make me," Lyric retorted, tossing her freshly installed bundles over her shoulder in a challenge.

Diamond lunged forward, her glass slipping from her fingers and shattering on the marble floor. Gasps echoed through the ballroom. Blair grabbed Diamond's arm, holding her back.

"Not here," Blair whispered urgently. "Not like this."

Diamond's chest rose and fell with rapid breaths as she glared at Lyric. "Get her out of my event."

Lyric smirked. "Oh sweetheart, don't take your frustration out on me just because you chose to marry an NBA player, who are infamous for their inability to keep their dick in their pants."

Before more words could escalate the confrontation, Cameron stepped forward, positioning himself between the two women. His hand hovered near Diamond, not touching but ready to offer support.

"Listen, this isn't the time or place," he said, his gaze steady on Lyric's face. "Let's not do this."

Cameron shifted moving closer to his wife; in case he needed to interject. Diamond's fury pivoted from Lyric to Cameron, her eyes flashing at him. "This is your mess. Your indiscretion brought this parasite into our lives! None of this would have happened if my husband hadn't put me in this position in the first place!" she roared.

Cameron's face tightened, the muscle in his jaw clenched. "I know, and I regret it every day. But this is your night, Diamond. Don't let her ruin it."

"Ruin it?" Diamond scoffed. "This heffa ain't ruining shit," her neck twisted as the Queens, New York in her rose to the surface. "She doesn't have that power. You, however, my fuckin' husband gave this bird the ammunition she needed to try."

Her tone was a whip-crack, lashing out with years of pent-up hurt and betrayal. Around them, conversations had all but ceased, the crowd drawn to the spectacle like moths to a flame.

"Let's talk about this later, please," Cameron implored, pain flickering in his eyes.

"Later?" Diamond echoed mockingly. "There is no later, Cameron. This needs to end now."

Cameron stood silently, absorbing the impact of

Diamond's words, his expression one of resignation and sorrow. It was clear to all who witnessed the exchange that, although the party continued around them, within the circle of their conflict, the world had narrowed to just Diamond, Cameron, and the shadows of past mistakes that clung stubbornly to the present.

A hush fell over the gathering as two broad-shouldered security guards advanced through the crowd; their eyes fixed on Lyric. Cameron stepped back, giving them room. Diamond's chest heaved with silent breaths, her gaze never leaving her adversary. The guards stood next to Lyric, one on each side, Lyric sighed dramatically, adjusting her dress.

"Fine, I'll leave. But trust me, Diamond, you're not as untouchable as you think. Besides, you should be thanking me. If it wasn't for me, no one would even care about your redemption arc."

Lyric turned on her heel, the security guards taking her by the arms as she was smoothly guided towards the exit, the cameras flashing as guests whispered furiously among themselves.

Diamond watched, the tension in her shoulders easing with each step Lyric took away from her. As Lyric disappeared behind the closing doors, an audible sigh of relief swept through the room. Conversations tentatively resumed, glasses clinked, and the thrum of music found its way back into the collective consciousness of the partygoers.

The launch party, momentarily derailed by personal vendettas, began to reclaim its prior vibrancy. Diamond was determined not to allow the chaos to stop the event from being a success.

Diamond's eyes scanned the room, catching sight of herself in a mirrored wall—her reflection poised and determined. She turned back to the crowd, her mask of confidence restored by necessity. She resumed her role as the gracious host, her laughter a little too bright, her smiles a touch too wide. All the while, her gaze flickered toward the door, watching, waiting, the anger within her kept at bay by sheer willpower.

"Thank you all for your patience," Diamond began, her voice clear and resonant. Her audience turned toward her; drawn by the commanding presence she exuded. "Tonight is not just a celebration of a brand; it's a testament to what we can achieve when we refuse to be defined by our past."

A ripple of applause broke out, but Diamond raised her hand, asking for a moment more of their attention.

"Every piece in this collection tells a story." She continued, her tone impassioned yet controlled. "A story of struggle, yes, but also of triumph. Of empowerment through adversity. This is for every woman who has ever been told she's too much or not enough."

Heads nodded in agreement, and the room swelled with a collective energy, a shared understanding that transcended the fabric of the garments being celebrated.

"Let's embrace our complexities, our flaws, and our unique strengths. Together, we are unstoppable."

The crowd erupted into cheers and applause. Diamond's heart swelled with pride as she stepped down from the spotlight, her speech lingering in the charged air. She retreated to a quieter corner of the venue. Here, she allowed herself a moment to just breathe, closing her eyes and feeling the weight of the evening temporarily lift off her shoulders.

"Quite the speech," a voice said from behind her, both familiar and unexpectedly soothing.

Diamond opened her eyes to find Marcus leaning against the wall, a half-smile playing on his lips. His presence was a balm to her frayed nerves.

"Thank you," she replied, her voice softer now, away from the crowd. "I meant every word."

Marcus pushed off the wall and took a step closer, his gaze holding hers with an intensity that made her pulse quicken. "I know you did," he said. "That's what sets you apart, Diamond. Your authenticity. It's... compelling."

She felt a flush creep up her neck at his words. There was a tenderness in his tone that she rarely encountered—especially from men in her world. "You always know what to say to make me feel better," she admitted, allowing herself this small vulnerability.

"Only because it's the truth." Marcus' hand moved as if he wanted to reach out to her but thought better of it, letting it fall back to his side. "You've turned this night around, despite everything. That takes resilience."

"Resilience built from years of practice," Diamond said, a hint of bitterness seeping through before she could stop it.

"Or maybe it's just who you are. Strong, even when you're standing in the middle of the storm." His voice was laced with something that sounded like admiration, and it sent a thrill through her.

Their eyes locked, and for a long moment, neither spoke. Diamond found herself drawn to him in a way that both excited and scared her.

"Maybe," she whispered, breaking the silence. "But

sometimes, I wonder what it would be like to weather the storm with someone by my side."

"Someone who understands what you're fighting for," Marcus added softly, finishing her thought.

"Yes," Diamond breathed. "Someone exactly like that."

They stood there, in the quiet corner of the bustling event. The world outside their intimate bubble continued on, but inside, something new and fragile was taking root—a deepening bond that promised strength and understanding in the face of whatever lay ahead.

Diamond pivoted gracefully from the quiet sanctuary she had found with Marcus, her stiletto heels clicking on the polished floor as she re-entered the pulsating heart of the launch party. She threaded through the clusters of guests. Women, influential and aspirational alike, reached out to her, their hands clasping hers, their words weaving a tapestry of congratulations.

"Your vision is revolutionary, Diamond," one executive said, her eyes alight with respect. "You're not just selling a brand; you're leading a movement."

"Thank you," Diamond replied, her voice smooth as silk. Each affirmation, each nod of approval, fortified her resolve, reminding her why she had embarked on this journey in the first place.

"Girl, you've got the Midas touch," another chimed in, her statement punctuated by a playful wink. Diamond's laughter mingled with the crowd's, a sound that felt both foreign and familiar in its genuine warmth.

Influential women continued to praise *Shine Like a Diamond* and its empowering message. The evening swirled around her, a kaleidoscope of success and solidarity, until finally, she found herself beside Cameron, Blair and Kirk.

"You did it!" Blair said, her smile as bright as the sparklers that had adorned the celebratory champagne bottles. "Despite everything. You really did it."

"Thank you. I only wish Kennedy could've been here to see my vision come to life. But she did send me the most beautiful bouquet of flowers," Diamond smiled.

"Yes, she was so disappointed she had to stay in LA, but her spirit was here with us," Blair reached over and gently touched Diamond's hand.

Cameron's gaze met Diamond's, a silent storm of emotion passing between them. There was regret there, and hope, in equal measure. "I'm really proud of you. You are an amazing woman, mother and wife," he said, his voice low but steady.

Diamond allowed herself a moment to bask in the glow of her accomplishment, feeling the weight of the night's challenges transform into a crown of victory upon her head.

The laughter and music swelled in the grandiose venue, a symphony of success wrapping around Diamond as she navigated through the crowd. A glass of champagne found its way into her hand, the bubbles mirroring the effervescence of the evening. She sipped, letting the crisp flavor tickle her tongue, and her gaze swept across the room—landing on Marcus.

Their eyes locked, a silent conversation unfolding in the space between them. There was a shared understanding. Diamond's heart fluttered, as they were two dreamers on the precipice of something new, something exhilarating.

"Here's to looking forward," Marcus mouthed across the distance.

"Here's to new beginnings," Diamond whispered back, more to herself than to him. The words were a vow, a quiet pledge to the journey ahead, one she would embrace with open arms and a spirit emboldened by every obstacle she had overcome.

Diamond turned away from Marcus, allowing herself a moment of introspection. She thought of the roads traveled, the bridges burned and rebuilt, the love questioned and rekindled. Each struggle had carved out the woman she was now, standing tall amidst a garden of achievements. But as she stood in the center of the ballroom, surrounded by luxury and success, Diamond's victory felt hollow. Because no matter how much she built, the cracks in her foundation—her marriage, her trust— were still there. And tonight, the world had just seen them up close.

As the chapter closed on the launch party, the final glance between Diamond and Marcus lingered, a testament to the myriads of stories waiting to unfold.

Chapter Eight

Turn Up A Notch

Kennedy leaned back in her chair, staring at the glowing screen of her laptop. A slow, satisfied smile spread across her lips as she scrolled through the confidential tax records she had obtained.

Lyric revealing that Darcy and Michael used her to create a fake charity for money laundering—both for their own gain and for clients—truly unleashed Pandora's box. This was merely a glimpse into the extent of their broader illegal operations.

Darcy and Michael had been cooking the books for years—fraudulent write-offs, offshore accounts, and enough shell companies to make even the most seasoned IRS agent salivate. It was everything she needed.

Lyric's fear about ending up in a federal prison ultimately compelled her to disclose some valuable information. That little nugget of professional misconduct was sufficient for Kennedy to uncover a large-scale tax fraud operation. Her fingers danced a meticulous ballet over the keyboard, punching in the final keystrokes to rollout phase one of her plan to release the sordid web of Darcy and Michael's *'alleged'* financial deceit.

She picked up her phone and dialed a contact. "It's time. Leak it."

Within hours, a bombshell report surfaced on major news outlets, accusing Darcy and Michael of potential financial crimes. Social media erupted with speculation. Kennedy watched with satisfaction as chaos unfolded in real time.

With a decisive click, she minimized the spreadsheets, their secrets now woven into the fabric of her master plan. The dimly lit office felt more like a war room than a workspace, yet it was here where Kennedy waged her silent battles.

Phase one, complete.

But she wasn't done. Kennedy had also planted false information about one of Darcy's biggest celebrity clients, a rising pop star known for her squeaky-clean image. An anonymous source claimed the singer was involved in a secret drug scandal. Kennedy crafted a narrative, a delicate anecdote poised to ripple through the upper echelons of the music industry elite. With deft keystrokes, she planted the seeds of a story so salacious it could only cling to the fringes of credibility—just enough to ignite the fuse of gossip without leaving her fingerprints on the match.

"Extravagant parties veiled in secrecy. A celebrity embroiled in an illicit affair, indulging in hard drugs" she whispered to herself, spinning the lies with skilled finesse. Her PR expertise came into play as she selected the perfect anonymous blog, a notorious hub for the juiciest urban whispers that skirted the edge of libel without ever crossing it. The post was live with a single click, and Kennedy leaned back, the ghost of a triumphant smile curving her lips.

As dawn broke over the skyline, the rumor had already spread rapidly across the city flickered with the breaking news, each iteration more embellished than the last. The internet was in an uproar. Michael's sleek office at his LA law firm and Darcy's office at Glitz Inc, were both engulfed in turmoil. Phones screamed incessantly, and the air buzzed with tension thick enough to slice. Their various teams, once a well-oiled machine of corporate precision, now scrambled in desperation, trying to patch the leaks in their rapidly sinking ship. Darcy rushed to do damage control, but the harm was already irreversible. Sponsors threatened to pull deals, and the pop star publicly distanced herself from Darcy's firm. Glitz Inc. was on the verge of crumbling.

"Who leaked this? How did they even get this information?" Darcy's voice cut through the pandemonium, sharp as shattered glass. Her usually impeccable poise unraveled with every passing second her empire threatened by the specter of disgrace.

She paced her office, phone glued to her ear, barking orders, "I don't care what it takes! Kill the story, spin it, bury it!"

But the damage was spreading faster than they could contain it, a wildfire of speculation and scorn consuming their carefully curated image. Employees whispered in huddled groups, eyes darting with the fear that their jobs were now on the line. Colleagues were making desperate gestures to calm the clients, the feverishly typing of emails intended for damage control, and the noticeable trembling of Darcy's hands despite her attempts to keep them steady.

"Everything I've built..." Darcy started, her voice trailing off, unable to finish the thought. She turned away, her resolve steeling her for the battle ahead.

Kennedy stood in front of the mirror in her office, adjusting the lapels of her blazer. Victory was so close she could taste it. Her phone vibrated against the polished surface of her desk, an unexpected interruption slicing through her thoughts. She glanced at the caller ID and recognized the number immediately.

"Kennedy," she answered, her voice exuding the confidence she now possessed.

"Hey, it's Omar," came the reply, his voice tinged with an urgency that sent a ripple of anticipation down her spine. "I've got news. Darcy and Michael are reeling, clients are pulling out, investors are asking questions, and board members are demanding answers."

A slow smile crept across Kennedy's face as she sat down in her chair, allowing herself this rare moment of satisfaction. The plan she had orchestrated was unfolding perfectly, each domino falling with precision. "My day is only getting better," she said simply. "Keep me updated."

"Will do," Omar confirmed before ending the call. In her high-rise office, sunlight poured through the floor-to-ceiling windows, casting a golden glow. Kennedy stood up looked out over the city that had tested her, taught her, and now awaited her triumphant return to the throne of Glitz Inc. With a deep breath, she savored the feeling of reclaiming control over both the company she had founded and her own life.

Darcy paced her penthouse, her usual refined demeanor slipping.

"That bitch set me up!" she hissed. "First the tax fraud leak, and now she's poisoning my clients against me!"

Michael sat across from her, his expression grim. "I have no intentions of being brought down by some second-rate publicist. We will hit back. Hard."

Darcy's eyes gleamed with malice. "Kennedy's got skeletons too. And if she wants a war, we'll give her one."

The next day as Kennedy was in the conference room preparing for a meeting, her phone buzzed ominously on the mahogany conference table. She picked it up, her eyes narrowing as she read the message that flashed across the screen.

"Nice move, Kennedy," the text from an unknown number began, oozing with menace. "But remember, skeletons don't like closets. They prefer the spotlight of public scrutiny. Back down, or we'll make sure your dirty little secrets join the party."

The message was a virtual grenade tossed in the midst of her triumph—a reminder that Darcy and Michael wouldn't go down without clawing at her foundations, trying to bring her alongside them into the abyss of scandal.

Kennedy's heart pounded against her ribcage. She could almost hear the ticking of an invisible clock, each second reverberating with the echoes of her past mistakes. Her initial elation morphed into a cold stone of dread settling deep in her stomach. The personal risk, the threat to her reputation and everything she had rebuilt looming.

But as Kennedy sat alone in the conference room, the weight of the choices before her anchoring her to reality. She had clawed her way out of obscurity, help build remarkable careers for others and resurrected her own from the ashes of public disdain once before. She would not be intimidated into submission. Not now, not ever. Her past was checkered, yes, a mosaic of triumphs and transgressions, but it was also the crucible that forged her tenacity.

She paced the length of the conference room, her mind a whirlwind of potential fallout. Yet, amidst the chaos of her thoughts, there was an unyielding core of determination. Losing Glitz Inc. again, after all the sweat and tears she had poured into it, was not an option.

"Threaten all you want," Kennedy whispered to the empty room, her voice a low growl of defiance. She had played the game long enough to know that fear was a weapon only if you allowed it to pierce your armor. And hers had been forged in the fires of adversity, impenetrable to the likes of Darcy and Michael.

Her reflection gazed back at her from the window—a woman who had risen from her own ashes, fierce and undaunted. This was more than a power struggle; it was a war for redemption—for herself, her agency, and her circle of loyalty. She had built her empire on the rubble of her past, and she would not cede her throne to threats or fear.

"Let them try," she fumed. Kennedy had survived worse. She could outmaneuver this too. Her fingers brushing over the threatening message one last time before she deleted it.

Kennedy arrived at the private lounge where she'd arranged to meet Lyric. The dim lighting cast a soft glow on the plush sofas, but there was nothing comforting about the tension that crackled in the air like static. She sat on the sofa across from Lyric. The reality star had a cocktail in hand, her perfect color-block nails tapping against the glass.

"Lyric," she said, her voice slicing through the hush, "we need to talk. You have a lot of nerve showing up at Diamond's event like that," Kennedy said coolly, crossing her arms.

Lyric smirked, sipping her drink. "What? I just wanted to celebrate a fellow boss babe."

"Save the bullshit. You knew exactly what you were doing."

Lyric set her glass down, leaning in. "And what are you gonna do about it?"

Kennedy cut her eyes at Lyric. "Diamond is a very close friend of mine."

"And I'm your client," Lyric smacked.

"You being my client can change. My friendship with Diamond won't. So, stay out her way, Lyric. I have no patience for your desperate stunts."

Lyric chuckled. "Oh, honey, I think we're both playing the same game."

Kennedy's gaze darkened. "That's where you're wrong. We're not playing the same game. Trust, you don't want to get in the mud with me. I advise you to watch yourself."

Lyric seemed to take the warning and addressed her with a new tactic. "Kennedy," Lyric began, her words cautious and measured, "the incident at Diamond's event wasn't what you think."

"Then enlighten me," Kennedy demanded, perching on the arm of the sofa opposite Lyric. Her protective instincts were flaring like caution signals in the night.

Lyric's fingers curled around the stem of her glass. She took a deep breath, and for a moment, the facade of the untouchable socialite cracked, revealing the raw vulnerability beneath.

"It was self-preservation, Kennedy. You know how this world works – eat or be eaten. I heard whispers, received disturbing letters, threats against my life... I panicked." The confession hung heavy between them, and Lyric's gaze dropped to the floor.

Being on a reality show had damn near turned Lyric into a professional actress, so Kennedy wasn't sure if this was a performance. Until she knew for sure, Kennedy allowed her anger to thaw.

"Who's threatening you Lyric, and why did you think Diamond had anything to do with it?" Kennedy's voice softened; it was no longer an interrogation she wanted to know if Lyric was telling her the truth.

"If there's anyone who'd want me dead, it's Diamond," Lyric rationalized. "I humiliated her globally by leaking that video, so of course she was among the top three suspects for those threats on my life. Doesn't matter now," she muttered, brushing it off with a flick of her wrist. "I made a mistake, Kennedy. I shouldn't have crashed Diamond's event."

"I was under the impression you didn't know who released that sex video. But, after it came out, you joined forces with Darcy to use it as a springboard for fame," Kennedy probed.

"That's mostly accurate. I assumed it was probably my ex-boyfriend being an asshole and released it on some revenge porn type shit," Lyric shrugged, taking another sip of her drink realizing she was talking too much and revealing more than she intended.

"I see. Well, I think we're clear that Diamond is off limits. Besides, we have more pressing concerns. Look, we both know Darcy and Michael are gunning for us," Kennedy said, her tone resolute. "Our main focus should be safeguarding your career and ensuring you stay out of prison, all while bringing them down."

"Kennedy, you know I'm all in. Darcy and Michael have been playing dirty for too long, and it's time for them to be put in their place. I might have severed a few connections on my way to the top, but I refuse to let those two bullies destroy everything I've worked for. It will be lovely watching their arrogant asses crash and burn," Lyric said with a mischievous grin. Kennedy nodded, feeling both confident and reassured that Lyric was completely committed to the downfall of Michael and Darcy.

Chapter Nine

Crossroads

The heavy iron gates of the state penitentiary groaned open, a sound that reverberated through Packer's bones like a dark harbinger. He surveyed the area, narrowing his eyes to shield them from the glare of the sun—a free man with the heart of a caged beast hungry for vengeance.

Packer stepped out of the prison gates, inhaling his first breath of freedom in months. The moment his feet hit the pavement; his phone buzzed. Vaughn and Lamar were waiting. He slid into the black SUV idling nearby, his crew welcoming him with nods of respect.

Long time, brother," Vaughn greeted him with a clenched jaw and fist bump, his eyes scanning the perimeter with practiced caution.

"You ready to handle business?" Lamar asked.

Packer's lips curled into a sinister grin. "I'm ready to kill that bitch, if that's what you mean."

Vaughn and Lamar knew Lyric had betrayed Packer, and he wasn't the type to forgive.

As the city moved on, unaware of the bloodshed that loomed, Packer and his crew began discussing the foundation that had already been laid for their most merciless scheme yet.

"Lyric thinks she's safe," Packer sneered, feeling the weight of their gazes on him. "She thinks I've forgotten."

"Nobody forgets," Vaughn grumbled, his voice rough. "Not something like that."

"Plan?" Lamar asked, his succinct question cutting through the tension.

"Them letters done already been delivered, now we destabilize," Packer outlined, every word deliberate, laced with malice. "Once she's scrambling, we strike. Have ya got in touch wit' her homegirls yet?"

"We found the three stooges. Them silly broads up to the same hoe shit. They down for whatever," Lamar laughed.

"Don't underestimate them hoes. Taj, Monroe, and YaYa gon' lead us right to that bitch." Packer stated with disdain. "Lyric Nunez," he spat the name like a curse. "When I'm done, everyone will remember why they feared the name Packer."

As the group gathered tightly together, their shadows blended into a single, menacing figure silhouetted against the peaceful city skyline.

Blair scrolled through her phone, her breath catching as she saw the notifications flooding in. Overnight, a single photo from her latest shoot had gone viral, sending the internet into a frenzy. It wasn't just any photo—it was *the* photo. A sultry black-and-white shot where her gaze smoldered into the camera, exuding power, allure, and untouchable confidence. It had been reposted by major fashion accounts, celebrities, and industry power players. Her name was on everyone's lips.

Her phone buzzed again—her agent.

"Blair, you are *everywhere* right now," her agent Gerad, gushed. "Campaign offers, brand endorsements, runway invitations—it's insane!"

Blair exhaled deeply, overwhelmed by the sudden wave of success. "This is surreal."

"It is. Plus, the first behind-the-scenes photos from your Savage X Fenty Valentine shoot have also just hit social media. Even the world's most efficient PR machine couldn't have orchestrated this anymore perfectly. The internet is on fire," Gerad shouted, his voice brimming with excitement.

"Wait...what? When did that happen?"

"About an hour ago. I have another call coming in, probably about you. I'll be in touch soon," Gerad said before ending the call.

As soon as Blair hung up, she immediately checked her phone. There it was—the behind-the-scenes photos, accompanied by a headline full of speculation. "Blair and Skee: Rekindling the Flame?"

"Fuck!" Blair put her phone down. The success she craved was happening, but the timing couldn't have been worse.

Just then, the door to her dressing room swung open, and Kirk stepped in, his expression a storm cloud of emotions. She could tell immediately—he had seen the pictures.

"You think this is cute?" Kirk snapped, his voice laced with frustration as he tossed his phone onto the table in front of Blair, displaying a gossip blog. "You letting the whole world think you're back with that clown?"

"Kirk, it was a job," Blair replied, trying to keep her voice even, to maintain the peace they had so carefully crafted lately.

"A job that just happened to pair you with Skee, your ex?" his tone was accusatory, the name itself a spark igniting the air between them. "You expect me to believe that's all it was? You didn't even tell me you did a photoshoot wit' him." the insecurity radiated from Kirk, and Blair could see the battle lines being drawn.

"Kirk, don't do this," she pleaded, her resolve starting to splinter. "Don't make this into something it's not."

"Am I supposed to sit back like a simp and smile while rumors fly about you rekindling a relationship wit' an old flame?"

"Rumors fueled by what? By jealousy? By your own insecurities?" Blair shot back, the frustration she'd been holding at bay surfacing like a storm swell.

"Jealousy?" he scoffed. "No Blair, concern. Concern for what this might do to us, to our family."

"Us?" her laugh was short, bitter. "I'm out there working, building a name for myself! And you—you're here fussing about meaningless whispers and gossip."

"Building a name, or rebuilding old relationships?"

Kirk fired back, each word a sucker punch to her to her resolve.

"Fuck, Kirk! Can't you see? This is my career, my passion. I can love what I do and still love you and our family."

"Can you?" he challenged, his jaw set as if bracing for impact. "Because right now, it seems like you can't tell the difference between past and present."

"Kirk—" Blair's voice broke, her armor cracking.

"Blair," he interrupted, softer now, but no less intense. "I support you; I do. But where does it end?" Kirk shook his head. "You out here playing dress-up with your ex while I'm holding it down at home. You know training camp is starting soon. Are you gon' let the nanny play mommy to our son while you continue to play dress up?"

"I'm not 'playing dress-up.' I'm building my career."

"At what cost?" his voice dropped, his eyes dark and demanding. "You need to make a choice, Blair. Me and our son... or this." He gestured toward the screen still displaying her and Skee looking like a power couple.

Her stomach twisted. "That's not fair."

"Life ain't fair," Kirk spit. "I'm done competing wit' your ambition."

"So, you can have your NBA career, but I can't follow my dreams."

"Again, at what cost? When do we come first?"

"Always," she whispered, the single word a promise, a plea, a testament to her internal struggle. "You always come first."

"Prove it." His words were a gauntlet thrown, and as Blair looked into his eyes, she saw not just the man she loved but the specter of a future on the brink.

"Kirk," she said, her voice steadying, "I will prove it. Not because you demand it, but because I want it. Because I want us."

"Blair, I want us too," he said, his voice a low rumble of contained emotion, "but you need to make a choice."

Her heart skidded to "A choice?" Her voice was barely audible a tremulous note in the midst of their domestic discord. Her chest tightened as if bound by invisible cords. Shock rippled through her, followed swiftly by a deep, aching hurt. She searched Kirk's face for any sign of the man who had once championed her dreams, but all she found were the hard lines of an unyielding stance.

"When we first went out on that double date with Diamond and Cameron, I mentioned wanting to be an actress. I felt embarrassed because I hadn't accomplished anything yet. But you told me, if that's what I want then I should go for it. You even accompanied me to my very first job Kennedy booked for me. You were incredibly supportive, unlike my boyfriend at the time, Michael. Now you're asking me to choose," she said softly, her voice strained with emotion. "My career, it's part of who I am."

"Then maybe we're not who you need." His words were cold, final, and they struck at the very core of her being.

"You're giving me an ultimatum?"

Kirk's expression hardened. "Yeah. I am." Silence stretched between them until Kirk finally spoke again. "I won't be second place to this industry, Blair. I won't let our son be either. He stepped closer, his voice dropping. "You have a choice to make. Either you focus on us, or you keep chasing this dream and lose everything."

He turned and walked out, leaving Blair frozen in place, her world crashing down around her. Blair loved Kirk, but she refused to shrink herself for him—or any man. She had fought too hard to carve out a space for herself. But the question that haunted her was one she had never dared to ask: Who was she without a man beside her?

After Kirk stormed out, slamming the door behind him, Blair exhaled a shaky breath. The battle between love and ambition had just begun—but this time, she wouldn't let anyone decide her worth except herself.

Later that evening, Blair sat in a private VIP lounge at one of the city's most exclusive clubs, nursing a glass of wine. The music thrummed around her, but she barely heard it. Her mind was stuck replaying Kirk's words, his ultimatum suffocating her.

Then, a familiar voice broke through her thoughts.

"Didn't think I'd find you here, Blair."

She looked up, and there he was—Skee, her former flame, the man who had once set her world on fire. He slid into the seat beside her, his eyes scanning her face.

"You good?" he asked.

Blair let out a bitter laugh. "Yes. I'm fine."

Skee studied her for a moment before reaching out, tucking a strand of hair behind her ear. "You forget—I know you. I know when you're putting on a front."

Her defenses wavered. She hated that he could see through her. That he still *knew* her.

"I just..." she exhaled, looking away. "Everything's

happening so fast. My career is taking off, but Kirk—he can't handle it. And now he's making me choose."

Skee's jaw tightened. "A real man wouldn't put you in that position."

Blair shook her head. "It's not that simple."

Skee leaned closer, his voice low and intimate. "It is, Blair. You destined to be a star, and anyone who genuinely cares for you will encourage your aspirations."

The words wrapped around her like a balm, soothing the raw ache inside her. She met his gaze, and for a split second, Blair forgot about everything—Kirk, the pressure, the ultimatums.

Before she could think, before she could stop herself, Blair moved closer. And so did Skee.

Their lips met in a slow, burning kiss. Familiar and intoxicating, a dangerous mix of past and present colliding.

The flash of a camera jolted them apart. Blair's stomach dropped as she spotted the lurking paparazzi, cameras pointed straight at them.

Her world had just exploded again—but this time, it was out of her control.

By morning, the internet was ablaze with scandalous headlines:

"Blair Dupont Caught Kissing Ex Skee Patron— What About Kirk?" "New It Couple or Career Suicide?" "Blair and Skee Spark Controversy" "Kirk McKnight's Heartbreak—Blair's Betrayal Caught on Camera..."

Blair sat frozen in her penthouse, scrolling through the chaos. Social media was in an uproar and the keyboard gangsters were ruthless. Some calling her a wannabee celebrity to a deplorable mother and crucifying her for betraying Kirk.

Her phone rang. It was Gerad.

"What the hell did you do, Blair?" Gerad's voice was sharp. "You know how bad this looks?"

Blair closed her eyes wishing that when she opened them, she would discover it was all a bad dream. "I didn't plan it. It just... happened."

"Well, now you have a full-blown PR crisis. Kirk hasn't made a statement, but you better believe he's going to."

As if on cue, Blair's phone buzzed with a notification. Kirk had just posted on Instagram:

"Some people chase fame, no matter who they hurt. I'll always put my son first."

Blair's heart dropped.

Then came another call. This time, from Kirk.

She hesitated before answering. His voice was ice-cold. "Pack your things, Blair. I want you out of the house by tonight."

The line went dead.

Blair's hands trembled as she placed the phone down. She had just lost everything.

Chapter Ten

Temptation

Diamond sat in her new office in Midtown Manhattan, her fingers dancing over the swatches of silk and satin, her gaze flitting across mood boards plastered with the vibrant hues of her new collection. She pinched a fabric sample between her nails, scrutinizing the way it caught the light.

"Perfect," she murmured, a smile playing on her lips as she envisioned models strutting the runway in her designs at the upcoming spring collection launch. This was her domain, a kingdom built from tenacity and flair, where every thread wove together stories of empowerment and elegance. *Shine Like a Diamond* was officially a success. This was the moment she had worked so hard for, yet a hollow feeling settled in her chest. It was Cameron—his face flickering into her thoughts unbidden, he was back on the road, the NBA season in full swing, and the whispers of doubt clawed at her sanity. She wanted to believe him when he said things had changed, that he was committed to their marriage, but the scars of betrayal ran deep. The stress of questioning his every move was suffocating.

She shook her head, trying to dispel the image, but it clung to her like a persistent fog. Doubts gnawed at her; mistrust lingered. Was Cameron truly committed or was their marriage another one of his games like he played on the court.

Diamond's emotional armor suddenly heavy upon her shoulders. She pressed her fingertips to her temples, the lines of worry etching deeper. Despite the gloss and glamor of her life, there were moments like these—raw, silent battles fought within the confines of her mind.

"Focus, Diamond," she whispered to herself, "You've built too much to crumble now."

She drew in a long breath, letting the air fill her lungs like a balloon stretching against the pressure. Her eyes closed momentarily, seeking solace in the darkness, a brief respite from the world she commanded. When she opened them again, her mind was sharp and clear, ready to withstand the pressures of her life.

"Let's get back to work," she said aloud, willing herself to erase her paranoia over Cameron.

A knock at the door broke Diamond's train of thought. Marcus stepped into her office. His presence brought a familiar comfort. His easy confidence and unwavering presence had been a source of contentment lately, more than she cared to admit.

"Looks like a hurricane of haute couture in here, Diamond," Marcus remarked with a chuckle." Diamond welcomed the distraction.

"Yes, it does, and I love it! Finally launching the fashion division is literally a dream come true," she enthused.

"It will no doubt be a huge success like everything else you've launched so far," Marcus said, placing a sleek tablet onto her desk, its screen alive with graphs and engagement metrics. "Shine Like a Diamond fashion is about to set off a storm all its own in the digital world."

Diamond smiled, "You always know how to spin chaos into strategy, Marcus."

They leaned over the tablet together, their heads close as they discussed hashtags, influencer partnerships, and viral marketing campaigns. His expertise in digital strategy was invaluable, and it showed in every click and swipe on the screen. His insights wove seamlessly into her vision, and together they crafted a narrative that would captivate their online audience.

"As much as I love our brainstorming sessions, there's something else I wanted to discuss," Marcus said, his voice taking on a more relax tone as he turned toward her, the professional veneer giving way to something more personal.

Diamond looked up from the screen, meeting his gaze. She saw something there—a flicker of emotion that wasn't just about business.

"Your resilience amazes me, Diamond," Marcus started, his words deliberate. "You're building an empire from a dream, and you stand strong even when the ground shakes beneath you. Not many can say they've done the same."

Diamond searched Marcus's face, looking for the intent behind his words. There was a depth there, a sincerity that reached out and wrapped around her heart, tugging gently.

"Thank you, Marcus," she replied, her voice softening. "That means a lot coming from you. You've been here since the beginning, seen the best and worst of this journey."

"More than just seeing, I've been...feeling," he added, carefully weighing his next words. "Feeling proud of what you've accomplished, feeling connected to your passion, feeling..."

He trailed off, seeming to search for the courage to continue. Diamond held her breath, sensing a confession lingering on the horizon.

Marcus reached across the polished expanse of Diamond's desk, his fingers grazing a stack of fabric samples. His touch lingered, but it wasn't the texture of the materials that held him captive—it was the proximity to her world, her essence.

"Feeling what, Marcus?" Diamond urged, her voice a blend of curiosity and something more fragile—like the first crack in a dam holding back a reservoir of unspoken truths.

"Feeling something for you, Diamond," Marcus finally said, his gaze locking onto hers with an intensity that sent a shiver down her spine. "More than just admiration. More than friendship."

Diamond's heart raced as she processed his words, surprise etching her features into an illustration of vulnerability.

"Marcus, I—" But words failed her.

As if sensing her turmoil, Marcus stood and made his way around the desk, closing the distance with a few measured steps. He stopped before her, his presence a gravitational force. She could feel the warmth emanating from him, smell the subtle scent of his cologne.

"Say something, please," he implored, reaching out to touch her arm. His hand was warm against her skin, grounding yet somehow electrifying.

"Marcus, this is unexpected," she whispered, her voice barely above a breath, her words betraying the truth. This wasn't unexpected, as she felt it too. "I don't know what to say."

"Then don't say anything," he murmured, leaning closer, so close that she could count the flecks of gold in his brown eyes.

Their breaths mingled, a tentative dance of inhalations and exhalations.

Her heart pounded as Marcus reached out, gently tucking a curl behind her ear, his fingertips grazing her cheek. Diamond closed her eyes at the touch, a sigh escaping her lips. It was a moment of surrender, of acknowledging something that perhaps had always been there, waiting for the right spark to set it aflame.

The pull towards him was magnetic, undeniable. She knew she should step back, break this spell before it wove itself tighter around them both. But for a heartbeat, or maybe an eternity, Diamond allowed herself to lean into the warmth, the promise, the perilous allure of what Marcus offered.

Diamond's hand trembled as she gently pushed against his chest, the warmth of his body searing through the fabric of his shirt like a brand. She took a faltering step back, her heel clicking sharply on the polished floor—a punctuation mark to the sentence neither of them wanted to end.

"Marcus, this... it's not right. I have to be true to my family," Diamond said, the resolve in her voice belying the storm of emotions swirling within her. Her heart raced with an illicit thrill, but the ring on her finger felt heavier now, a reminder of the vows she had made, the weight of her marriage crashing down on her.

Marcus exhaled heavily, nodding. "I'll respect that. But just know, I'm not going anywhere."

Later that night, Diamond sat alone in the quiet of her dimly lit living room, the soft glow of the city lights filtering through the translucent curtains. The day's events replayed in her mind. She rubbed her temples, feeling the pressures of her double life weighing down on her. Her marriage to Cameron, a man she fell madly in love with, seeing as her Prince Charming and lifeline, now seemed like a fortress under siege, with its foundations slowly eroding from doubt and mistrust. She loved him—she knew that—but love wasn't just a feeling; it was a choice, a commitment.

Diamond curled up on the sofa, hugging her knees close as the silence enveloped her allowing unwanted memories flood her mind. Even though it happened weeks earlier, Lyric crashing her launch event was the triggering factor that resurfaced Cameron's betrayal. She closed her eyes, searching for clarity amidst her mental chaos.

"Focus on what you can control," she whispered to herself. "Your brand, your legacy, your children." These were the anchors that kept her grounded when the tumultuous tides of her heart threatened to sweep her away.

Diamond realized that no matter how strong the pull towards Marcus, she couldn't let it capsize the life she had built. She needed to weather this storm, not only for herself but for her family. With a deep breath, she reaffirmed her decision, promising to steer her ship through rough waters with resilience and grace. She stood up, drawing the curtain back slightly, and peered out at the sprawling city below, a mosaic of light and shadow.

With a silent vow, Diamond turned from the window, ready to face whatever challenges lay ahead, even as the subtle hint of an impending storm lingered in the air.

Meanwhile, over in the Bronx, Packer was seated in the faintly lit backroom of a shabby club, flanked by YaYa, Monroe, and Taj. A cigarette smoldered between his fingers as he leaned forward, a sinister grin on his face.

"It's time," he said, his voice like gravel. "That hoe think she slick. She out here thinkin' she living her best life. Lyric 'bout to find out otherwise," Packer spit as he extinguished his cigarette. "I want that bitch gone. No loose ends."

YaYa shifted nervously. "So, umm when this going down? I mean, you sure you wanna do this?" she asked, wanting to discourage Packer from his diabolical plan. "Lyric famous. She got eyes on her now. Cameras, bodyguards—"

"I don't give a fuck," Packer bark. "She ain't untouchable. We'll hit her when she least expects it."

The tension in the room was suffocating. They had all seen what Packer was capable of. And now, he was out for blood.

"We ready boss. All you gotta do is let us know when," Lamar nodded, taking a gulp of Hennessy straight from the bottle. Monroe looked at Taj with regretful eyes. Despite YaYa's warning not to open the door when Packer arrived, she couldn't resist. Reminiscing about the generous payment they received for fucking Cameron and Kirk at that bachelor party a few years back consumed her mind with dollar signs. With rent overdue and other bills piling up, Monroe hoped Packer had another job for them. Indeed, he had a job opportunity, but instead of setting up a man, it involved luring Lyric into a trap.

YaYa exchanged nervous glances with Monroe and Taj, the weight of Packer's plan settling heavily on their shoulders. The reality of what they were about to do was sinking in, and the air in the room seemed to thicken with a sense of impending doom. The glint in his eyes sent a shiver down YaYa's spine, a premonition of the impending chaos.

"Packer, are you sure about this? What if something goes wrong?" YaYa's voice trembled, revealing her apprehension about the plan that would soon be executed.

Packer's laughter sliced through the tension like a knife. "Ain't nothing gon' go wrong if you all follow my lead," he sneered, his confidence bordering on arrogance. "This shit long overdue. That bitch was supposed to been dead."

YaYa knew what type of nigga Packer was, that's why she cautioned Monroe against opening the door and allowing him back in their lives. It had been over two years since Lyric left New York to chase her dreams of fame in LA, yet Packer was still out for blood. She wanted no part of his scheme but realized she was as good as dead if she didn't comply with his demands.

The air grew heavy with tension as Packer's words lingered, each syllable dripping with malice. YaYa, Monroe, and Taj exchanged uneasy glances, the weight of their involvement in Packer's sinister plan settling like a stone in the pit of their stomachs. They all knew the dangerous game they were about to play, but fear and desperation had clouded their judgment, trapping them in a web spun by Packer's diabolical scheme.

When Packer rose from his seat, a malevolent glint in his eyes, a sense of foreboding washed over YaYa. She knew there was no turning back now; they were all entangled in a deadly dance orchestrated by a man with no regard for human life. The room seemed to close in on her, the walls pressing closer with every heartbeat.

As the group in the Bronx continued to listen to Packer's sinister plot against Lyric, Diamond found herself tossing and turning in her bed, grappling with the emotions that Marcus' confession had stirred within her. The darkness of the night seemed to mirror the shadows creeping into her heart, blurring the lines between right and wrong, desire and duty.

Her phone buzzed with a text notification, cutting through the silence like a knife. Diamond hesitated for a moment before reaching for it, half-afraid of what message awaited her in the glowing screen. It was Cameron, his familiar name flashing across the display.

"Miss u already," the message read, accompanied by a string of heart emojis that once would have made her smile. But now, they felt like a cruel reminder of the fractures in their relationship, the unspoken doubts that lingered between them like ghosts from a past she couldn't quite let go of.

Diamond stared at the message for what felt like an eternity, her fingers hovering over the screen as conflicting emotions waged war within her. She wanted to reply, to reassure Cameron that everything was fine, that she missed him too. But the words stuck in her throat, suffocated by the weight of unspoken truths and buried resentments.

She knew she couldn't continue existing in this limbo, pretending that everything was fine when cracks had long begun to form in the facade of her marriage. As she lay in the darkness of her bedroom, Diamond made a silent vow to confront the turmoil within herself. The time for indecisions was over; she needed to face her truths head-on, no matter how painful they might be.

Chapter Eleven

Public Reckoning

The clock on the wall was ticking, its steady rhythm a stark contrast to the storm raging in Kennedy's mind. She hunched over her desk, framed by the glow of her laptop in the otherwise faintly lit office.

Her fingers paused mid-type, hovering above the keyboard as she replayed the consequences in her mind. This was more than a business move; it was a life altering decision that could topple her world as she knew it.

In the midst of her debating, without warning, the door burst open with such force that it seemed to suck the breath out of the space. Michael strode in, a dark silhouette against the hallway light. His eyes, sharp and unyielding, locked onto Kennedy instantly.

Kennedy barely had time to react when Michael walked into her office unannounced, his imposing frame blocking the doorway. His expression was calm, too calm, and that alone sent a shiver down her spine.

"We need to talk."

Kennedy sat up, keeping her expression neutral. "Michael," she greeted, her voice steady despite the adrenaline spiking through her veins. Her mind raced, calculating the distance between them. "There's nothing left to talk about. Glitz Inc. was mine, and you and Darcy stole it. That ends now."

Michael chuckled darkly, stepping closer. He stopped just short of her desk, his stance wide, a predator cornering its prey. A cold smile played across his lips, but his eyes remained devoid of warmth, mirroring the chill that wrapped around Kennedy's spine. "No, what ends is you. Drop this, Kennedy. Walk away, or you'll regret it."

She stood her ground. "Are you threatening me?"

His smirk faded, and in an instant, he grabbed her wrist, squeezing just enough to make his point. "I'm warning you. You continue down this path, I promise you won't like what happens next."

Kennedy yanked her arm away, fire burning in her eyes. "Do your worst, Michael. Because I'm done being afraid."

His gaze swept over her office, taking in the disarray with a contemptuous lift of his brow.

Kennedy squared her shoulders, fighting to maintain control of the room—and the upper hand in whatever game Michael thought they were playing. She wouldn't cower, not when so much was at stake.

"From the moment you inserted yourself into Blair's

life, promising her stardom, I knew you would be a problem. You think you're smart, don't you?" his voice was a low growl, barely more than a whisper, yet it carried the weight of an unspoken threat as he leaned in, his breath heavy with intent. "You're playing a dangerous game, Kennedy. Do you really think you can win against me?"

"I don't play games, Michael. Besides, I'm not the one with a trail of deceit behind me," Kennedy shot back, her voice cutting through the charged silence like a whip. She refused to let his intimidation tactics unravel her.

Michael's facade of calm cracked for a moment before smoothing over into a mask of indifference. "You have no idea what you're up against, Kennedy. And don't forget, you have your own skeletons. The power I hold can crush you without leaving a trace."

A bitter laugh escaped Kennedy's lips, laced with defiance. "I've faced worse than you and come out on top, Michael. You think your threats scare me? I've seen the darkest corners of ambition and emerged stronger."

His eyes narrowed, and in that moment, Kennedy sensed a shift in their deadly dance—this was no longer about mere threats. This was a declaration of war.

"Consider this your final warning," Michael hissed, his words cutting through the air with lethal precision. "Drop whatever you have planned next or suffer the consequences."

Kennedy's heart pounded rhythmically against her chest, yet her eyes remained unwavering, firmly meeting Michael's gaze. "Fuck you, Michael. It's time everyone saw you and Darcy for the foul, grimy duo you are. Now get out of my office before I call security."

Michael stepped back, the danger in his eyes was

unmistakable. He was a savage pushed to the brink, and Kennedy knew she had just become his most significant threat.

"Your righteousness could be your downfall," he warned, the menace in his tone now undisguised.

"Or it could be my redemption," she retorted, her voice steady despite the adrenaline coursing through her veins.

As Michael turned on his heel and stalked out of the room, Kennedy let out a breath she hadn't realized she'd been holding. She felt like a lone gladiator who had just faced down the emperor in the Colosseum — vulnerable yet invincible.

She stood motionless, feeling the aftershocks of his presence. Her fingers gripped the edge of her desk, the cool wood grounding her as she fought to steady her breathing.

"Get it together, Kennedy," she whispered to herself, closing her eyes to shut out the world. In the blackness beneath her closed eyelids, she resolved to battle no matter the cost.

That night, when Kennedy got home, her mind was still racing with Michael's threats and the weight of what she planned to do. The stakes had never been higher. When she entered the bedroom, she heard the water running, Sebastian was in the shower.

At first, Kennedy considered waiting until he was done so she could purge her soul, by laying out her fears and uncertainties. But the thought of talking, of explaining, felt exhausting. What she needed—what she craved—was something deeper. A release, an escape, a reminder of the one person who made her feel safe in a world full of betrayals.

She stripped off her clothes and stepped into the shower, the steam wrapping around her like a cocoon. Sebastian turned at the sound of the glass door opening, his eyes darkening with understanding the moment he saw her. No words were needed. He pulled her against him, his hands running down her slick skin, grounding her, consuming her.

Their lips met with urgency, a silent conversation of need and desperation. Kennedy melted into him as he pressed her against the tiled wall, his mouth tracing fire along her neck. Fingers tangled, bodies entwined, water cascading down as they moved together, erasing everything but this moment.

For a little while, the chaos outside didn't exist. There were no threats, no betrayals—only them. Only the love they made in the heat of the water, reaffirming something deeper than words could ever convey.

As they collapsed against each other, breathless, Kennedy knew the moment wouldn't last. But at least for now, she had this. She had him. After an intense sex session in the shower, they continued their love making in the bed. Kennedy became lost in their lust until drifting off to sleep in each other's arms.

The next morning, Kennedy's transition from the relative quiet of her office to the press conference was like stepping out of a silent snowfall into a hurricane. Each step toward the door, she could feel the pieces of her carefully constructed life shifting, rearranging into a new pattern she would have to navigate. But she was ready. She had to be.

Kennedy stood at a podium in front of a sea of reporters, cameras flashing as she prepared to lay it all bare. She paused for a moment, the air was thick with anticipation, every reporter ready to pounce on the scent of scandal. She felt their energy as a tangible force, pushing against her with the power of a thousand whispers turned into shouts.

Reporters jostled for position, their voices a blare of curiosity and demand.

"Ms. Harper! Ms. Harper, over here!"

"Can you tell us about the allegations—"

"Is it true that—"

She lifted her chin, her gaze sweeping across the room. In this moment, she was the maestro before the orchestra, the conductor of truth in a symphony of lies. The chaos around her stilled as she prepared to reveal the score she'd been silently composing.

"Thank you all for coming," Kennedy began, her voice cutting through the noise like a beacon. As she spoke, the gravity of her words anchored them to the silence that had bloomed in the wake of her presence. The truth was a heavy thing, but she bore its weight with the grace of someone who had finally found solid ground beneath her feet.

Kennedy's fingers curled around the edges of the podium. She leaned forward slightly, her eyes meeting those of the crowd before her.

"Today, I stand before you to shed light on the darkness that has shrouded the business dealings of Darcy Woods and Michael Frost," Kennedy's voice quivered just a fraction. "Darcy and Michael have engaged in fraudulent activities that threaten the very foundation of ethical and legal business practices."

A collective gasp rippled through the room, a wave of disbelief and intrigue washing over the reporters' faces. Kennedy's heart hammered in her chest, but she steadied her breath, anchoring herself in the eye of the storm she was unleashing. She continued to expose Darcy and Michael's tax fraud, their manipulation, and their dirty dealings, but she didn't stop there. With her heart pounding, she took control of the narrative. Kennedy's voice reached a crescendo, she turned the spotlight onto herself with unwavering honesty, revealing her own faults, mistakes that had haunted her in the dark of night, secrets that had gnawed at her conscience, betrayals, the cutthroat PR games she had played—all of it. The weight of her revelations felt like chains breaking free, the sound of liberation ringing loud and clear in the room.

Her admission hung in the charged air, raw vulnerability on display amidst the chaos. The truth was her armor now, and she wore it with a strength she never knew she possessed. The room buzzed with a fervor, the reporters scribbling furiously in their notepads, capturing every word for the headlines that would surely follow.

As the press conference came to an end, Kennedy felt a mix of relief and apprehension. She had unleashed a whirlwind of chaos that would surely ripple through the elite circles she once navigated with ease. As she anticipated the backlash was immediate. Some praised her bravery; others called her reckless.

Surrounded by a throng of reporters clamoring for more details. She answered their questions with poise and determination. From a short distance, Kennedy noticed Sebastian, who had always been her anchor. He watched in shock as the woman he loved detonated her entire world.

Later that night, Kennedy mentally prepared herself for an ambush when she entered their apartment, and Sebastian delivered.

"I don't even know who you are anymore," he said with contempt. "You didn't just take Darcy and Michael down—you burned everything to the ground, including yourself."

Kennedy swallowed hard, holding his gaze. "I had no choice. If I didn't control the story, they would have."

Sebastian sighed, running a hand through his hair, his expression a storm of frustration and hurt. "Nothing in you thought to tell me what you intended to do last night? You just send me a text this morning, telling me where to show up. I'm supposed to be your man, your partner in life. Why would you blindside me like that?"

"I'm sorry, Sebastian. When I came home, I planned to tell you. But for just one night, I wanted to be with you without thinking about Michael and Darcy, without the weight of everything crashing down on us. I just needed that moment with you," Kennedy explained, guilt threading through her resolve. "To be honest, I didn't fully commit to revealing the complete truth until I was standing right there in front of that podium."

Sebastian exhaled sharply, shaking his head. "What

you did was reckless, and that's how the world saw it. I'm caught in the crossfire. Did you even think about what this would do to us?"

"I thought about everything. And I chose the truth, no matter the cost."

"And now what? Now you're the villain, too. How am I supposed to trust you when you've kept so much from me?"

Her heart clenched, but she refused to back down. "I was wrong for not discussing what I intended to do with you first. For that, I sincerely apologize. But I did what I had to do. I need to be able to look at myself in the mirror. We might live together but I must be able to live with myself. And if you can't accept that, then maybe you don't really know me at all."

As Sebastian walked away, Kennedy realized the truth—winning came at a cost. And she had just lost the one person she thought she could hold onto. But there was no turning back now. The war had begun.

Chapter Twelve

$\mathcal{P}ower\ \mathcal{M}oves$

Blair sat on the balcony of her new apartment, staring out at the busy New York City street. The crisp night air bit at her skin, but she barely noticed. Her world had imploded in the span of days—Kirk had thrown her out, the media had branded her a homewrecker, and fans were either rallying behind her or tearing her apart. She had lost everything that once defined her. The glow of the screen was merciless, each notification a relentless hammer against her reality. It had been weeks and photos continued to swirl across her feed—her and Skee, entwined in an illicit kiss that now held her career and personal life hostage to public scrutiny. She sat frozen on the edge of her sofa, phone clutched like a lifeline, as her world threatened to implode in high definition.

Her thoughts drifted back to the last encounter with Kirk. She found herself revisiting their argument several times a day and today was no exception.

"Blair!" Kirk's voice slashed through her haze of disbelief, his anger leaving the room devoid of air.

She looked up, eyes wide, to find Kirk looming in the doorway, the muscles in his neck taut with barely contained fury. The atmosphere between them crackled, charged with a poisonous blend of betrayal and hurt.

"Kirk, please let me explain—" Blair started, her voice a frayed whisper, but he cut her off with a sharp gesture.

"Explain? How the fuck do you explain this?" He thrust his own phone at her, the image on the screen a mirror of her own nightmare. "You're all over the internet, Blair. What the hell were you thinking?"

She stood, the motion unsteady, as if her limbs couldn't bear the weight of her transgression. "It wasn't— it's not what it looks like. It was just a moment, a mistake."

"You've become nothing but a mistake for me," he spat, the pain in his eyes belying the harshness of his words. "How long has this been going on behind my back?"

"Nothing's been going on," she insisted, the desperation in her tone clawing at the walls of the room. "Skee and I, we just... It was a one-time thing. A lapse in judgment."

"Judgment?" Kirk laughed bitterly; the sound devoid of any real humor. "You think you can chalk this up to bad judgment?"

"Kirk, I love you," Blair pleaded, reaching for him, desperate to close the gap of mistrust that had widened between them.

He grimaced at her touch, stepping back as if burned. "Love doesn't humiliate you in front of the whole fuckin' world, Blair."

"Kirk, I'm sorry," she said, the words hollow, knowing they could never absorb the grief etched into his features.

"Sorry won't fix this shit." His voice was low, deadly calm. "It doesn't erase what everyone's seen... what I've seen."

"Please," she whispered, her heart fracturing with the realization of what she stood to lose.

"Get out," he said, and though his tone was quiet, it reverberated through her like a death knell.

"Kirk—"

"Get. Out."

The finality of his command left no room for argument. Her pleas died in her throat, swallowed by the gulf of his anger and the certainty that she had shattered something irrevocable.

When Blair first moved into her new place she sank down onto the bare floor, her arms wrapping around her knees. This wasn't just another residence; it was a tangible sign of her fall from grace, a self-imposed exile from a life she had cherished but now no longer existed. The uncertainty of what lay ahead loomed large, and for the first time in a long while, she felt truly alone, disconnected from the world that spun relentlessly outside her window.

She closed her eyes, taking a deep breath, trying to imagine a future beyond the scandal, beyond the pain of today. After doing that for a few weeks, slowly, Blair opened her eyes, her gaze settling on the blank canvas of walls that surrounded her. They were empty now, but they were hers to fill. With a tenacity that surprised even herself, she stood up, determination beginning to stitch together the tattered edges of her spirit.

No longer would she allow her mistakes to define her; she would reclaim her narrative, piece by painful piece. Blair knew the road ahead would be fraught with challenges, but as twilight bled into the cityscape, she felt the faintest spark of something she thought she'd lost... hope.

Her phone buzzed. It was the doorman. "Yes?"

"Gerad Lang is here to see you," the doorman's voice crackled through the speaker.

"Let him up," Blair sighed, she wasn't ready to face him, or anybody, but isolation was a luxury she couldn't afford.

Minutes later, Gerad swept into Blair's stark new reality—a far cry from the plush comfort of the home she'd been expelled from. Gerad was a shark in designer clothing, his eyes scanning the room, already calculating how to spin this new chapter of Blair's life.

"My dearest Blair, are you out of your mind? Your name is everywhere! You should be doing damage control, making some kind of sympathy play, not hiding out like some disgraced has-been."

Blair smirked. "Who said I was hiding?"

Gerad hesitated. "Well, I haven't heard a thing from you, and your kiss with Skee, it's gold darling. Scandalous, yes, but gold." He circled the room like a predator closing in. "We've got interview requests from every major network. I'm talking legacy media. They're ravenous for your side of the story."

"Intriguing," Blair thought, as her mind started to

turn over ideas.

"Think about it, Blair. Redemption narrative, the misunderstood heroine... We spin this right, and you're back in the game. Bigger than ever."

"Or I become the villain in my own story," Blair countered, her voice low but firm. "Book me interviews. Big ones. And tell the brands that dropped me they're about to regret it."

"Interesting..." Blair could see the wheels spinning in Gerad's head.

"I've spent years playing by the rules, trying to be the perfect girlfriend, the devoted mother, the respectable good girl image. And where has that gotten me? Tossed aside the second I did something everyone deems is wrong. No more. If the world wants a scandal? I'll give them one."

"I like it. No! I love it! Circa Rihanna Good Girl Gone Bad era. I'll start working on that immediately!" Gerad's eyes gleamed with excitement at the idea of transforming Blair's new good girl gone bad image."

"Not just yet. I need to decide what I want my next move to be," Blair replied, contemplating her options.

"Remember my love, we can't keep the people waiting. If we don't strike soon, they'll be on to the next scandal, so do hurry," Gerad gave her a curt nod, assured of his persuasive skills, and then exited, leaving Blair alone to strategize her next course of action.

Blair sank onto the bare mattress that now served as her bed. She struggled with deciding what would be her best option. She longed for empowerment, to rise from the ashes of scandal and reclaim her place in the face-paced world where relevance was currency. Yet, she feared feeding the voracious appetite of the public's eyes and losing herself in the process, becoming nothing more than a character in a drama scripted by others.

Surveying the empty room, Blair's determination began to intensify. Regardless of the outcome, she was adamant that the direction she took her career would be hers alone to make. She now held the pen that would write her story, even if no one approved of the ending.

Lyric was lounging in her Beverly Hills penthouse, scrolling mindlessly through her phone when it rang unexpectedly. It was a number she didn't recognize. She hesitated, debating whether to answer, but curiosity got the best of her.

"Hello?"

"Lyric, girl! It's me YaYa."

Lyric sat up straight, her heart skipping a beat. "YaYa? Damn, it's been a minute. How did you get this number?"

YaYa laughed lightly. "Come on now, you know I got my ways. I had to reach out. I miss you."

Lyric chewed her lip, suspicion creeping in. It had been years since she left her old life behind in New York, and she hadn't kept in touch with anyone from that world. Not after what went down with Packer. "Miss me? Or just miss what being around me can do for you?" she asked, her tone cautious.

"Come on, Lyric. It ain't even like that. We grew up together. I know we lost touch, but I just miss my homegirl. No drama, I swear."

There was a long pause. Lyric didn't trust easily, and for good reason. But a part of her did crave the familiarity of home, to reconnect with the people who knew her before the fame, before the reality shows and the headlines. She let her guard down. "Maybe we can grab dinner or something next time I stop through New York. But if you're bringing drama, I'm out."

YaYa forced a smile through the phone. "No drama, I promise."

As soon as the call ended, YaYa exhaled shakily and turned to Monroe and Taj, who sat across from her at Packer's hideout.

"She bought it," YaYa muttered. "She wants to meet up next time she's in New York."

Monroe nodded, but her expression was troubled. "I don't know about this, YaYa. Lyric was our girl. And what Packer's talking about? That's cold-blooded."

Taj folded her arms, eyes darting toward the locked back room where Packer was making his latest plans. "You think we gotta choice? We say no, we'll end up on Packer's bitches to kill list."

YaYa swallowed hard, guilt heavy in her chest. She had reached out, pulled Lyric in under the guise of friendship, and now she was leading her into a trap.

"We just gotta play it smart," YaYa whispered, her voice unsteady. "I'm not trying to be the next body he buries. But maybe—maybe there's a way to warn her."

Monroe and Taj exchanged a worried glance. They all knew one thing for sure—Packer wasn't the kind of man you double-crossed and lived to tell the story.

It took a few weeks, but Blair was ready to execute her plan. She strutted into a known celebrity packed nightclub wearing a red silk dress that clung to every curve. The second she entered, all eyes turned to her. Conversations stalled. Phones lifted. She was no longer Kirk's ex-fiancée. No longer the fallen star. She was *the* moment.

At the VIP section, Skee Patron lounged with his entourage, a knowing smirk spreading across his face as she headed towards his booth. "Damn, Blair. You sure you wanna add fuel to the fire?"

Blair slid into the seat next to him, plucking a glass of champagne from the table. "The fire's already burning," she said smoothly. "Might as well dance in the flames."

The cameras flashed. The headlines were already being written.

By the following morning, Blair had officially re-branded herself. Gone was the demure, picture-perfect image Kirk had once demanded of her. In its place stood a woman unapologetically embracing her fame, her desires, her *power.*

She appeared on every major talk show, flipping the scandal on its head.

"Did I kiss Skee? Yes," she admitted on *Good Morning America.* "But let's stop pretending women can't make mistakes without being vilified. Men leave their wives and start a whole new family with another woman, and people don't blink an eye. It's time we stop expecting women to be perfect."

Her boldness was polarizing, but the risk paid off. On every social media platform, her following tripled. Brands clamored to sign her again. The *Blair Dupont Redemption Tour* was in full effect, and at the center of it was a woman who had taken her lowest moment and spun it into her greatest comeback. Blair was no longer asking for permission. She was taking.

Chapter Thirteen

Showdown

Diamond stood in the striking, sun-drenched 53.5-foot great room of their penthouse located in the heart of SoHo. The space exuded a unique blend of indoor and outdoor oasis, thanks to a distinctive sliding wall of windows that opened onto the wrap-around terrace.

There was almost 1,600 square feet of beautifully landscaped outdoor space wrapping around two sides of their home, with a private park and a custom endless pool right off the living room.

She reminisced about the day Cameron purchased the penthouse just after they decided to keep their family intact and rekindle their marriage. It was meant to symbolize new beginnings. Cameron spared no expense

when acquiring what appeared to be the perfect masterpiece. The custom Bulthaup kitchen featured stain-
less steel cabinets, Thassos marble countertops outfitted
with a suite of Miele and Gaggenau appliances. The main
bedroom wing occupied the entire southwest corner of
the penthouse. The suite had private access to the terrace and an entire dressing room with 12 custom closets.
It was serene and luxurious, with the primary bathroom
having heated floors, a free-standing cast iron tub, and a
separate steam shower stall. Additional highlights included custom walnut built-ins, handmade Belgium bronze
hardware, and a private mud room. The 14 story, ultra-
luxury, white glove condominium building also included
amenities such as a 24-hour doorman and concierge, private garage with valet parking, health club with a Pilates
center, and a 50' lap pool. It was the epitome of New York
dream living.

The couples lavish surroundings couldn't conceal
the suffocating tension between them. A striking contrast to the fresh start they had imagined when they first
settled into their brand-new luxurious home. Here was
Diamond, in the center of Manhattan, facing the rift that
had formed in her marriage. Her heels echoed on the
quarter-sawn white oak herringbone floors as she approached her husband to address the potential demise
of their marriage.

"Cameron," Diamond began, her voice a tremulous
mix of grit and raw nerves. "We need to talk...about us."
She halted in front of him, swallowing hard as she met his
gaze. "I can't keep pretending everything's okay."

The plush sofa held Cameron in a casual embrace,
but his posture tensed as Diamond's anxiety-laden words

filled the space between them. Trust that should flow effortlessly between them only had this sultry air of uncertainty.

"Baby, what's wrong?" his voice was a subdued thrum of concern.

"Everything!" Diamond's hands fluttered to her chest, as if to quell the rapid beat of her heart. "I know it was weeks ago, but the confrontation with Lyric brought back all these old wounds. They've left scars, Cameron. And I'm struggling to recover." Her eyes searched his, seeking an anchor in the storm of doubt that Lyric's betrayal had stirred up.

Cameron rose from the couch, his movements slow and deliberate as he closed the distance between them. His expression eased; the lines of remorse carved more pronounced lines as he observed the anguish on his wife's face.

"Diamond, you know I love you, right?" his fingertips grazed her arms, bringing with them a warmth that felt both familiar and distant. "I haven't—wouldn't ever—break our vows again."

She wanted to believe him, more than anything, but the ghosts of deception cast long shadows. "I need more than words, Cameron. We need help." Her voice broke over the last word, betraying the depth of her vulnerability.

"Then we'll get help," Cameron conceded. "I'll do whatever it takes. Counseling, therapy... anything to rebuild what we have. To rebuild your trust." He cupped her face, thumbs gently wiping away the moisture brimming in her eyes.

"Promise me," Diamond implored, allowing herself

to lean into his touch, craving the reassurance of his presence even as her mind wrestled with doubt.

"I promise, Diamond." Cameron affirmed, his vow ringing with the gravity of the commitment he was making. "I'm all in. For us."

As Diamond nestled into the crook of his arm, a fragile hope blossomed within her. Perhaps, their love could find a way to thrive amidst the turmoil. The road to healing would be long and uncertain, but for now, she allowed herself to rest in the solace of his pledge.

Lyric arrived in New York for a series of business meetings, but after the unexpected call from YaYa, she decided to carve out time for her childhood friend. They met at an upscale restaurant in Manhattan, the kind of bougie spot Lyric never would have stepped foot in back when she ran with YaYa, Monroe and Taj. The restaurant exuded an ambience of opulence and exclusivity. The air was filled with the rich aroma of truffle oil and caviar, mingling with the scent of expensive perfume and cologne.

The lush velvet chairs cradled patrons as they dined, with smooth, cool touch of marble tabletops. It was a place for those who could afford to spend their money frivolously, and who delighted in the extravagant and ostentatious. The place screamed luxury and snootiness, with rich fabrics and elegant decor adorning every inch. The type of establishment that whispered of wealth and privilege, a far cry from the gritty and raw streets that Lyric and YaYa used to rule. But things had changed.

YaYa greeted Lyric with an enthusiastic hug, squeezing tight as if trying to galvanize the past. "Girl, you look amazing! Hollywood's been good to you."

Lyric relished in the compliment, sitting down. "It has its perks. You know I always knew I was meant for more than just the block."

YaYa chuckled, but there was something forced about it. "I ain't mad at that. I'm proud of you. I mean you got me eatin' at some top-notch shit," she remarked glancing at the chandeliers hanging from the ceiling, mirrored walls and the menu that was embossed with gold lettering. "I know you footing the bill," she laughed.

"Girl, you know I got you," Lyric winked.

The conversation drifted between old memories and casual updates, but Lyric, despite the warmth of nostalgia, felt a slight unease she couldn't shake. "So, tell me, why now? Why reach out after all this time?"

YaYa took a careful sip of her wine, then shrugged. "I been thinking about getting out of New York. I see you making moves, doing big things. Figured maybe it's time I switch things up too. My business has dried up in New York. Maybe I can come work for you."

Lyric leaned back, tilting her head. "You serious?"

"Very. Yeah, it's a fact, I always thought I was the shit, but time has humbled me. You a star and I would be honored to work for you," YaYa beamed, knowing that flattery was still the key to opening Lyric's lock.

"You know what...I do need a new personal assistant. I fired the last one a few weeks ago. She was my third hire in three months. Good help is hard to find. No one seems to understand me," Lyric complained, rolling her eye.

"No one understands you better than me, your

childhood bestie. I still remember that you love ketchup on your scrambled eggs."

Lyric's eyes widened with glee. "Bitch, you are hired!"

The two women clinked their wine glasses together.

"I can't wait! Just let me know when I start, boss," YaYa winked.

"After I leave New York, I'll be in Miami for a few weeks, handling some business. Once I get settled, I'll fly you out. There's a grand opening of a high-end strip club there, and I've been hired to host. It will have exclusive VIP clientele. The type of place that prints money. Of course, I need my personal assistant right by my side."

YaYa's smile widened. "Let me know when and I'll pack my bags, 'cause there's no other place that I wanna be."

Lyric, feeling a rare sense of trust, reached across the table and squeezed YaYa's hand. "Then consider yourself invited as not only my personal assistant but my special guest. Fresh start for both of us." They once again clinked their crystal glasses in celebration.

Kennedy stormed into the sleek glass office of Glitz Inc., her heels clicking sharply against the marble floor. The entire building was in chaos—employees whispered in frantic huddles, the phones rang endlessly, and a noticeable tension thickened the air. Darcy's empire was crumbling before everyone's eyes, and Kennedy had come to finish the job.

Darcy stood near the floor-to-ceiling window, arms

crossed, her normally pristine appearance slightly disheveled. Her jaw was tight, but she exuded the same arrogant confidence that had made her such a formidable opponent.

"Well, if it isn't the woman of the hour," Darcy said, her voice dripping with venom. "Come to gloat, Kennedy?"

Kennedy smirked, tossing a thick manila folder onto Darcy's desk. "No, I came to collect what's mine. You stole Glitz Inc. from me, and now, you're going to give it back."

Darcy picked up the folder and flipped through the damning documents inside—emails, financial statements, offshore accounts, all proving the fraudulent schemes she and Michael had orchestrated. Her face darkened as she threw the folder down, glaring at Kennedy.

"You think you've won?" Darcy scoffed. "You think you're just going to waltz back in here and take over?"

"I don't think, Darcy. I know," Kennedy shot back, stepping closer. "You've got two options," she declared, tossing another thick folder onto the desk. "Sign the company back over to me, or I take every piece of dirt I have on you and Michael straight to the authorities. And trust me, after that press conference, the Feds are already circling."

"You can't strong-arm me. You and I both know this business doesn't survive on morality. You want it back? Fight me for it."

Kennedy stepped closer, voice a razor's edge. "I already did. And you lost. Your name is mud, your clients are fleeing, and Michael is one subpoena away from a prison cell. Do you really want to go down with him? Or do you want to cut your losses and walk away with whatever dignity you have left?"

Darcy let out a dry laugh, shaking her head. "Oh, Kennedy... you are so naive."

Kennedy folded her arms. "Enlighten me."

"You really think you're untouchable? You really think your hands are clean? You and I both know you've done dirt, and if I go down, I'll make sure you go down with me."

Kennedy's expression hardened. "I own my mistakes. That's why I went public. The difference between us? I tell the truth; you hide behind lies."

Darcy's lips curled into a wicked smile. "You want the truth? Fine. Let's talk about your friend and client, Lyric, who I know is responsible for feeding you the tax information about me and Michael."

Kennedy narrowed her eyes. "What about her?"

Darcy picked up a pen from her desk, twirling it between her fingers as she feigned boredom. "Well, let me give you a little truth bomb of my own. You ever wonder how Lyric got Cameron on that sex tape? The footage that made her a star? It wasn't some wild night of passion. She set him up."

Kennedy stiffened. "What are you saying?"

Darcy sat down in her chair leaning back, her voice barely above a whisper. "She drugged him."

A stunned silence filled the room. Kennedy's stomach twisted as she searched Darcy's face for any sign of deceit, but all she found was smug satisfaction.

"That's a damn lie," Kennedy spat. "You want to ruin Lyric's career with this bullshit narrative because your life is in shambles."

Darcy shrugged. "Believe what you want. But Lyric knew exactly what she was doing. She needed a scandal to launch her career, and what better way than to expose an NBA Superstar and humiliate his wife in the process. Diamond...your very close friend," Darcy mocked. "How does Diamond feel about you repping the woman the world saw fuck her husband?"

Kennedy shook her head, disbelief washing over her. "You're just trying to manipulate me. There's no way Lyric would—"

"Wouldn't she?" Darcy cut in. "She was desperate. Her deadbeat boyfriend Packer had nothing to offer. She did what she had to do to survive."

Kennedy's mind reeled. If this were true, then everything—Diamond and Cameron's marriage imploding, Lyric's rise to fame, the scandal that rocked the industry—had all been built on a well-orchestrated scheme. But did Lyric even have the wits to pull this off on her own. Kennedy wasn't convinced.

"You have no proof," Kennedy insisted, her voice uncertain.

Darcy smirked. "Oh, but I do. Friendly reminder, Lyric was my client first. And if you push me any further, I'll make sure the whole world knows Lyric's shocking secret."

Kennedy's breath hitched. This changed everything. If she handed all the evidence she'd gathered on Darcy and Michael to the authorities, she risked taking down Lyric too. The weight of that truth crushed down on her.

Darcy leaned back in her chair, smugly satisfied. "Tell me Kennedy, are you really willing to burn everything down, including your client? She's a huge reality star now, even has her own show thanks to you and the PR firm you work for."

Her mind whirled with conflicting emotions, torn between her loyalty to Diamond and the unsettling revelation about Lyric. Kennedy clenched her fists. She had fought too hard to get here. But now, the battle was messier than she had ever anticipated. The revelation about Lyric sat like a stone in her chest. She met Darcy's gaze head-on, her voice cutting through the heavy silence like a sharp blade.

"If what you say is true, then Lyric will have to face the consequences." Kennedy then reached across the desk, grabbed the legal documents she had prepared, and shoved them toward Darcy. "But nothing has changed. Sign the damn papers."

Darcy laughed coldly. "You think you have all the power, don't you?" she hesitated, her jaw tight, but she knew she was out of options. With an icy glare, Darcy snatched the pen but refused to scrawl her name on the dotted line.

"Listen you raggedy bitch, I won't let you manipulate me into sacrificing everything I've worked for. Glitz Inc. is mine. When I return to this building, those papers better be signed, your shit better be packed, or I'll pack it for you. But either way, you will be getting the fuck out," Kennedy warned as she turned to leave.

Chapter Fourteen

Calculated Rise

Diamond sat in her office headquarters. It was a sanctuary of calm. The gentle hum of the city below filtered through the closed blinds. Sitting behind her glossy mahogany desk she stared out the window at the glittering NYC skyline. The success of her brand should have been fulfilling, but her mind was elsewhere—on Cameron, on her fractured marriage, on the betrayal she still couldn't shake. A familiar dread settled over her. The late-night calls became sporadic, his messages grew shorter, and old wounds reopened. No matter how much success she built, the uncertainty of her marriage gnawed at her.

A soft knock at the door pulled her from her thoughts. Marcus stepped inside and stood by the window; his athletic frame silhouetted against the fading light. He turned, his eyes filled with concern. "You, okay? You seemed off at the event earlier." He moved closer, his face etched with compassion. "Talk to me, Diamond. What's going on?" his voice was a soothing balm, but the turmoil inside her resisted easy healing.

Diamond sighed, "It's just...everything." Her eyes lifted to meet his, shimmering with unshed tears. "Cameron and I, we've been sinking. And I spoke to Kennedy the other day and there's talk that Lyric drugged him. It's all too much." She swallowed hard, struggling to maintain her composure. "We agreed to attend couples counseling but..."

"But what?" Marcus positioned himself in front of her, hesitating for a moment before placing a comforting hand on her shoulder. "You don't have to hold back. I'm here for you."

"The problem wasn't just him having sex with Lyric," Diamond went on. "Yes, the video being made public was the ultimate humiliation, but Cameron had cheated on me before, which created trust issues. Now that he's back on the road for the NBA season, I'm afraid he'll betray me again," she confessed. "What if he can't change. I don't know if the temptations are too strong, and he'll cheat once again."

"Diamond, your husband should never make you question his loyalty. Maybe it's time to stop waiting for him to change."

She turned to face him, her heart pounding. "It's not that simple. We have history. A family."

Marcus searched her face. "But are you happy? Do you feel loved the way you deserve to be?"

Tears welled in Diamond's eyes. "I don't know anymore."

Marcus lifted a hand, brushing a stray tear from her cheek. "You deserve someone who sees you, who values you. Not as someone's wife, but as you. Diamond, the woman."

The chemistry between them was undeniable. The tension that had simmered for months boiled over as Diamond closed the space between them. Her lips met his in a slow, hesitant kiss, then deepened as a rush of emotion took over. His hands found her waist, pulling her closer as they lost themselves in the moment.

With the city lights glowing behind them, Diamond let go of her doubts—just for tonight. She needed to feel something real, something undeniable. And in Marcus's arms, she finally did.

Their kiss deepened, fueled by attraction, passion and vulnerability. Diamond's heart raced with the thrill of something new, something unburdened by the weight of her failing marriage. She knew this was wrong, that she was betraying Cameron in a way similar to how he betrayed her, but Diamond didn't care. She pulled Marcus closer. In this moment, she allowed herself to forget the chaos of her life, relishing in the warmth of his touch.

Marcus lifted her effortlessly, placing her on the edge of her desk. His lips trailed along Diamond's neck, igniting a fire that had been buried beneath years of heartbreak. She gasped as his hands explored her body with a tenderness and passion she hadn't felt in so long. She let herself surrender, let herself feel something real, something powerful.

Clothes slipped away, bodies pressed together, the

world outside disappearing as they gave into the inevitable. Their movements were slow at first, filled with longing, before turning desperate and consuming. Every touch, every kiss, was a silent promise that this moment belonged to them alone.

As Marcus whispered her name against her skin, Diamond knew there was no turning back. And for the first time in a long time, she didn't want to. In his arms, she felt wanted, cherished—alive.

As the first light of morning streamed through the office windows, Diamond awoke in Marcus' arms, torn between guilt and exhilaration. She couldn't deny that the sex had been amazing. Although uncertain about what this meant for their relationship, she knew she craved more.

Blair sat in the hotel suite, her reflection staring back at her from the vanity mirror. She was perched on the edge of an overstuffed armchair, her silhouette bathed in the soft glow of a single table lamp. Shadows clung to the corners of the room, creating an ambiance that felt both intimate and foreboding. The weight of the upcoming interview pressed down on her chest, but she refused to break. This was her moment—not to clear her name, but to own it.

"Be real, be raw," she murmured, rehearsing the mantra that had become her anchor in the tumultuous sea of public scrutiny. "The truth is your power."

"Ms. Blair Dupont, can you explain..." The immaterial question from her mock interview hung in the air, unanswered, as the recording paused.

"Can I?" Blair whispered to herself, her determination warring with the dread that clutched at her throat. This wasn't a friendly chat that contained softball questions like her sit down with Good Morning America. This was an in-depth interview for a feature article in Vanity Fair. She was about to press play once more when the door creaked open.

Diamond and Kennedy entered, their presence cutting through the tension like a refreshing breeze. "I'm so happy you all are back," Blair sighed, sinking into the armchair.

"Girl, you look like you're about to face the firing squad," Diamond said, her voice rich with warmth and cheerfulness as she approached her best friend.

"More like laying my soul bare for the world to pick apart," Blair replied, offering a half-smile.

The women flanked her, "We're here. No need to worry." Their expressions serious as they prepped her for the no-holds-barred interview.

"Blair, you have to be strategic," Kennedy advised, crossing her arms. "This isn't about apologizing. It's about controlling the narrative. You're not the victim. You're the powerhouse who survived."

Diamond nodded in agreement. "You need to own it, but don't let them twist your words. Give them just enough to satisfy their hunger but not enough to tear you apart."

Before Blair could respond, Kennedy's phone buzzed. She glanced at the screen and frowned. Another anonymous message. Without a word, she opened it, her breath hitching as her eyes scanned the text.

"You ladies survived death once. But your luck has run out. We're watching. You can't escape it again."

Kennedy's grip on the phone tightened. "Survived death," Kennedy repeated.

Blair and Diamond exchanged worried glances as Kennedy turned the screen toward them. Unlike the previous vague threats, this message seemed much more personal.

Diamond exhaled sharply. "Who the fuck is doing this? Survived death. What is that even about?" Diamond was utterly confused.

"Hold on. Could they be referring to the shooting at your mother's funeral?" Blair asked, suddenly looking alarmed. That tragic day felt like a lifetime ago, and the women rarely discussed it.

"Blair, you might be right because we've never spoken about the incident publicly. We were all there, and when those bullets rang out, I genuinely thought we might die," Kennedy admitted.

"I felt the same way," Blair nodded.

"So, you think someone from my mother's funeral has been sending us these horrible notes and text messages," Diamond shook her head.

"I planned to bring it up later, after my interview, but yesterday, someone left a note with my doorman. I arrived just seconds after the envelope was dropped off. I rushed outside to see who it was but only managed to catch a glimpse of them getting into a car before it sped away," Blair recounted.

"This is insane!" Diamond exclaimed as she started pacing the floor of the hotel suite. "No one has ever been arrested for my mother's murder, and the police never found out who opened fire at her funeral."

"What if... what if it's all connected? The shooting at

the funeral, these threats... what if they're linked somehow?" Kennedy's eyes widened.

Blair's heart pounded in her chest as the pieces started to fall into place. The sense of violation she felt surged through her veins.

Diamond stopped pacing and fixed her gaze on Blair.

"This is getting out of control. We need to find out who's behind this before it escalates even further."

"Maybe I shouldn't do this interview," Blair murmured, more to herself than to Diamond or Kennedy. "I thought doing this interview would allow me to take control of the narrative. And give the middle finger to Kirk, and everyone else trying to portray me as the villain, but maybe all this press I've been getting, is putting a target on us."

"Blair, no." Diamond's voice was firm. "You can't let whoever this is win. You've worked too hard to get here." Diamond leaned against the armrest of Blair's chair. "You're gonna kill it, just like you do everything else."

"Exactly. And remember why you're here," Kennedy said, tucking a loose strand of hair behind Blair's ear. "You have an opportunity for your voice to be heard. Own your shit. Your truth is your armor."

"Let's go over the tough questions one more time," Blair said, feeling the tightness in her chest loosen ever so slightly.

Together, they delved back into preparation, but that stopped by the jarring ring of a cell phone. Blair fumbled in her purse, retrieving the device.

"Hello?" Blair's voice was cautious.

"Blair, it's Gerad." Her agent's tone buzzed with an excitement that felt worlds away. "You're not going to believe this—Cassidy Holt wants you for the lead in his next film!"

A surge of elation rocketed through Blair's veins, so potent it nearly eclipsed the fear that had taken root moments earlier. Her career was at a crossroads. The scandal left which path she should follow questionable, but now this lifeline appeared, giving her a definitive answer. Cassidy Holt—a notorious Hollywood director, infamous for pushing boundaries, saw potential in her. His name alone carried the weight of Hollywood royalty, synonymous with box-office gold and career-defining performances. Him offering her the lead role in a high-stakes drama could redefine her entire career.

"This isn't just another role, Blair," her agent gushed over the phone. "This is the kind of movie that catapults you from influencer to A-lister."

Blair took a deep breath. "Are you serious?" she finally managed to say, her eyes widening as Diamond and Kennedy leaned in, their expressions morphing from anxiety to anticipation.

"Dead serious. They saw your screen test, and they're convinced you're the one. This is huge, Blair."

The room seemed to spin; the possibility of a star-making role was everything Blair ever dreamed of a chance to cement her spot among the stars of the silver screen.

"Gerad, this is incredible," Blair stuttered, overwhelmed by the news.

"So, is that a, yes?"

"Of course! But I'll call you back. I have to get ready for my Vanity Fair interview." Blair ended the call, her hand trembling as she placed the phone on the table sharing the incredible news with her two best friends.

Diamond squealed, throwing her arms around Blair. "You see, this is your moment!"

Kennedy's smile was more measured, but her eyes shone with pride. "Blair, this will be life changing."

"I know and I'm scared," Blair confessed.

Diamond stepped back to look Blair squarely in the eyes. "Fear is good. Use it as your source of power. And remember, all of the great changes taking place is because you've earned it."

Kennedy nodded in agreement. "You're not the same person you were just a few months ago. You're stronger, smarter."

"Going ahead with the interview, doing this role... it's me taking control, isn't it?" Blair's determination fully on display.

"Exactly," Diamond affirmed, her gaze unwavering. "You own your story, Blair. No one else."

"Okay." Blair took another deep breath, letting the certainty of her friends' belief wash over her. "Let's do this."

After a chaotic week, Blair was looking forward to spending some quality time with Skee away from the limelight. Escaping the madness for just a few stolen moments in the privacy of his home was exactly what she needed. Blair found herself drawn back into Skee's orbit; their chemistry undeniable. Now that her relationship with Kirk had completely unraveled, she wondered if returning to her past might be the key to her future. Skee had become her refuge, her safe space. He stood wrapping his arms around her, offering solace, a sweet distraction from the pressures and expectations placed upon her.

"You look like you ready to conquer the world," Skee greeted her, his deep silky voice able to soothe her soul.

"When I'm with you, I do feel that way," Blair smiled, as they sank into the plush couch, her head resting on Skee's shoulder.

"Tell me what's been going on. Everything," Skee urged. "I wanna hear about this new Hollywood role that's gonna make my baby a superstar."

As Blair recounted the details of what had transpired the last few days, Skee listened intently. Their conversation was a fluid dance of words. Blair found comfort in expressing her ambitions in Hollywood, free from the judgment she often faced from Kirk. It was invigorating to have a man in her life who fully supported her dreams.

She leaned into his embrace, her eyes drifted toward the balcony, where she noticed a small group of people outside mingling on the expansive terrace.

"I thought we were alone," Blair said, pulling away from Skee's embrace.

"Babe, I'm sorry. Once you came, I almost forgot anybody else was here. You remember my friend Packer?"

"No." Blair shook her head.

"He just stopped by for a minute wit' some of his crew. Let me get them outta here so we can have some alone time," Skee said, kissing Blair on the forehead before making his way to the terrace.

"I'ma need ya to finish up them drinks and head out so I can spend some time wit' my girl," Skee told Packer when he stepped out on the terrace.

"I understand man," Packer glanced over at Blair from a distance. "Spendin' time wit' yo' woman is important. Now that I'm back on these streets, I gotta get me one," he chuckled.

"If a woman will keep you outta trouble, get one quick," Skee joked. "But real talk, I'm glad you stopped by man. I want you to keep your head straight. I got something for you—be my road manager on tour." Skee propositioned. "I don't wanna see you going back to prison."

Packer smirked, knowing his mind was already elsewhere—locked on revenge. "I got you. I'ma stay clean," Packer lied.

While Skee stood talking to the small group of people on the terrace, Blair instantly remembered Packer, as he was unmistakable with his stocky figure, broad shoulders and air of self-importance, but it wasn't him that caused the tremor in her spine. Blair's pulse quickened as she scanned the scene, her gaze landing on another man standing beside Packer. He made her stomach twist in knots. Recognition hit her like a freight train. The sharp cut of his jaw, the predatory lean in his posture, it all flooded back with chilling familiarity. She had seen him before. The sender of those poisonous notes was just a few feet away.

The evening the doorman gave her the last threatening note, she had caught a glimpse of someone running away from her apartment. It was him. Blair also recalled the figure approaching with a gun threatening to end her and Diamond's lives. Though his face was concealed, the same sensation she felt then washed over her now as she looked at the man with Packer. Her blood ran cold.

Skee was laughing with them, completely unaware

of her growing panic. Was he involved? Did he know what was happening?

She forced herself to stay calm, not wanting to alert anyone to her suspicions. But she immediately sent a frantic message to Diamond and Kennedy.

I think I know who's behind the threats. And it's worse than we thought.

She became consumed in her thoughts and what she should do next.

"Blair?" Skee's voice tethered her back to reality. "You okay?"

"Fine," she lied smoothly, but her heart was racing. She hesitated, caught in an internal tug-of-war. To confront Skee now, to demand answers, or remain silent. She stole one last glance over his shoulder. The man had turned, his eyes a pair of dark wells that seemed to stare straight through her.

There were pieces missing, a puzzle half-formed, and she needed to see the whole picture before making her move.

"Something on your mind?" Skee asked, his voice a gentle probe.

"Always," she said with a wry smile, her gaze fixed on Skee. For now, she decided she would wait.

"Hey," Skee said, reaching out to gently touch her arm, sensing the shift in her energy. "Whatever it is, you're not alone in this." His gaze held hers, earnest and reassuring. Skee still had this way of pulling Blair in.

"I apologize, but I just got a message from Diamond. She's dealing with some personal issues and needs me there immediately," Blair said, grabbing her purse and keys.

"You have to leave right now?" Skee asked, worry in his voice. "I'll go with you," he offered, not wanting to be separated from her.

"Thanks, but I really need to do this alone. I promise I'll call you later."

Blair hurried out, leaving Skee unnerved.

Chapter Fifteen

It All Falls Down

Kennedy and Diamond were devouring the pineapple spicy guacamole, beef birria tacos and wild mushroom quesadilla at Anejo Tribeca when Blair arrived. The clatter of silverware against porcelain and the muted conversations of nearby diners blended into an ambient symphony as Blair explained her encounter at Skee's penthouse while sipping on her rose sangria. She leaned forward, elbows on the table, her gaze flitting between Diamond and Kennedy with a seriousness that drew them in.

"I know Skee and Packer are childhood friends, but the other guy, I swear he is the one that almost shot us at your mother's funeral," Blair insisted staring at Diamond.

"I also believe it was him that left the envelope with my doorman and sending these threats to us."

Diamond's brow creased with worry, her fingers drumming on the linen tablecloth. "Blair, honey, this is no small thing. If Skee's involved with Packer, he could be dangerous," she cautioned.

Kennedy, always the thinker and strategist, tapped her lips thoughtfully with a slender finger.

"I doubt Skee had anything to do with it. He was at the funeral, standing right beside me when the shots rang out. He could have been hit just as easily. Everything happened so quickly, and both gunmen had their faces concealed. Skee might be entirely unaware of what's happening. We need to consider every angle. How can we connect Packer's friend with the notes and text messages? And if it is him, why target us?"

"That's an excellent point, Kennedy," Diamond agreed. "Skee might not be a part of it but if the guy you saw is in Packer's crew, then Packer has to know. But what would Packer have against us?"

"Fuck!" Kennedy blurted, placing her fork down just as she was about to take another bite of her food. "Packer is Lyric's ex-boyfriend."

"What?!" Blair and Diamond shouted in unison.

"Yes!" I completely forgot that Lyric and Darcy mentioned it to me. After releasing that sex video, she packed up and left Packer behind in New York to chase fame in LA."

"Lyric had sex with my husband," Diamond nodded.

"And one of Lyric's friends also had sex with Kirk. I saw that video myself courtesy of Skee, who he got from Packer," Blair added.

It was all starting to click. The waiter brought a plate of chicken empanadas, but the food went unnoticed as the trio dove into speculation.

"Unfuckin' believable. Could Packer be responsible for my mother's death but why?" Diamond was puzzled.

"Maybe your mother wasn't the intended target?" Blair mused, pushing her untouched plate away.

"Shit, Cameron and Kirk." Kennedy voiced what Diamond and Blair were thinking.

"What kind of twisted game is Packer playing, and how do we prove it?" Diamond interjected, her anger simmering beneath her words.

"We need to dig deeper into Packer's past, see if there are any loose ends that tie back to us," Kennedy asserted. "If Lyric left him after the scandal with the sex video, he might have a grudge against anyone connected to her or those who knew about it. This could be his twisted way of seeking revenge."

Diamond listened intently to Kennedy, and suddenly, everything became clear with a chilling clarity. "If he's willing to go this far, who knows what else he's capable of?" Diamond's protective instincts flaring up.

"We have to stay one step ahead of him. If Packer is behind all this, we need to collect evidence while moving with caution. He and his crew are dangerous," Blair said with a sense of urgency to unravel this mystery before more harm could be done.

As YaYa was packing for their flight to Miami in the morning, Monroe and Taj was standing in front of the mirror dancing and rapping along to **Whatchu Kno About Me by GloRilla & Sexyy Red:**

It's a Friday night (What's up?)
My nigga ain't at home (Let's go)
I pour my bitches shots (Uh-huh)
'Cause I'on drink alone (Hell nah)
I'm outside again (Let's get it)
'Cause, bitch, I hate at home (Da fuck?)

It's giving hair, face, ass, titties (Woo, aye, ugh, yeah)
Hair, face, ass, titties (Woo, aye, ugh, yeah)
It's giving hair, face, ass, titties (Woo, aye, ugh, yeah)
Hair, face, ass, titties, (Woo, aye, ugh, yeah)...

"Bitch, this song is makin' me wanna hit the club!" Monroe shouted as she grinded her hips to the beat.

"I don't understand how ya in here shaking yo' asses, with all the bullshit that's about to go down," YaYa shook her head, pacing nervously in between packing her clothes.

Taj turned the music down and sat on the bed. "Girl, me shaking my ass is the only thing keeping me sane right now. I don't want no part of this bullshit, but we don't have no choice," she huffed.

"We still have time," Monroe chimed in. "If we warn Lyric now, she could disappear."

YaYa bit her lip. "And if Packer finds out? We're dead."

Taj sighed, rubbing her temples. "Maybe we play both sides. Give her just enough info to be on guard, but not enough for Packer to suspect us."

YaYa clenched her fists. "I do wanna figure out how to get outta this. This job Lyric offered me would give me a fresh start. And I'm sure she can find something for you all to do to," she reasoned.

Taj and Monroe exchanged glances as they considered what it would be like being a part of Lyric's Hollywood lifestyle.

"We have a decision to make, and we need to make that shit now," Monroe contended.

There was a loud banging at the front door making the women immediately stop their intense conversation. "I bet that's Packer," Monroe said, getting up to let him in.

Monroe hesitated for a split second before opening the door, her heart pounding in her chest. As she swung it wide, Packer's imposing figure filled the doorway, his sharp gaze immediately honing in on the tension in the room.

Packer surveyed them with a predatory stare, each second stretching into an eternity under his scrutiny. His smirk widened as he appraised them with cool detachment. "I was dropping by to see if my little birds are ready for our flight tomorrow?"

"Yes, Monroe and Taj already have their bags packed," YaYa said, glancing over at their luggage in the corner. "I'm finishing my packing now."

"Good. I don't need you silly hoes fuckin' nothin' up. In a few short days, Lyric will be a dead bitch. If she's not, then the three of you will be," Packer warned.

YaYa, Taj, and Monroe shared an ominous reality. They knew he wasn't bluffing—his threats were as real as the danger lurking behind them. None of them were ready to die behind this bullshit, but they didn't want to be responsible for Lyric's death either. Fear clung to them like a second skin, with the uncertainty of how Packer's sinister plan would unfold. His menacing presence loomed over them, suffocating any remnants of loyalty they had left.

Diamond faced Cameron in his man cave, nervously drumming her fingers on a glass of wine, her other hand resting on her hip while the city skyline shimmered behind her like a restless blend of streetlights and shadows. The tension between them was thick. Cameron was fresh off a long road trip, exhausted, but the look in Diamond's eyes told him that sleep was the last thing on his agenda tonight.

"I have to ask you something, and I need you to be honest with me," Diamond's voice heavy with unspoken demands.

Cameron sulked, shaking his head. "What is it now, Diamond? Another argument?"

"No. Tell me about Packer," she said, watching his reaction closely. "I need to know everything about your history with him. No lies."

Cameron tensed at the mention of the name. He leaned back, exhaling sharply. "Packer... we never ran in the same circles, why are you bringing him up?"

"So, you're saying you don't know him?" Diamond's grip on her glass tightened.

"That's not what I said. We used to gamble at the same spot Uptown. But I didn't fuck wit' him. We actually exchanged words a few times and one time almost came to blows. But I backed away, 'cause he was on some reckless dumb shit. I ain't have time for that," Cameron shrugged. "But you still haven't told me why you askin' me about Packer. I ain't heard his name in forever."

"I know there's more than what you're telling me," she pressed, her eyes boring into him, searching for the smallest flicker of truth.

Cameron sat on the edge of the leather couch. He shifted, the soft leather creaking under him as his eyes traced the expensive patterns in the Persian rug as if it might give him the answers he needed.

"Diamond, I don't know what the fuck else you want me to say. Why are you bringing that man up to me?"

She took a step closer, "Because I came across some information a few days ago."

"What kinda information would you come across that would involve Packer?"

"Because I think he had something to do with my mother's death, and the shooting at her funeral."

Cameron's eyes widened; surprise evident on his face. "Hold the fuck up. How do you go from us having beef because I beat him a couple times gambling to killing yo' mother and then the shooting at her funeral? You really think he'd do some foul ass shit like that?"

"I know he would," she said firmly. "You can't think of any reason why he would have a vendetta against you?" Diamond asked in an accusatory tone.

Cameron hesitated. "I don't know. I mean, yeah, Packer and I had some bad blood, but nothing that should've led to murder."

"Did you know Lyric was Packer's girlfriend when she made that sex video with you?" Diamond pressed, inching closer. Each step a drumbeat to her growing impatience.

"Wait...what? This is crazy." Cameron rose from the couch, placing his hand on his forehead, pacing the room in disbelief. "If what you're saying is true, we have to handle this before it escalates."

Diamond carefully observed her husband's reaction and felt confident that it was sincere, that all the details she had just shared were news to him. She nodded. "Right now, all I have are suspicions. The police will need much more than that to make an arrest for my mother's murder."

"I can't wrap my mind around such trivial bullshit resulting in your mother being murdered and the shooting at her funeral," Cameron fumed, his frustration simmering into rage. He clenched his fists.

"I'm convinced my mother was never the intended target. Packer sent those men to eliminate you, and she got caught in the crossfire. They returned to finish the job at her funeral, and fucked that up too," Diamond reasoned. "I'm certain that he's linked to her death, and some recent subliminal threats that's been occurring."

Cameron clasped his head with both hands, besieged by forces beyond his control. "I can't believe your mother is dead because of me," he mumbled in utter disbelief.

The room seemed to close in on them, the towering windows providing no escape from the harsh reality. Diamond could feel her own heartbeat, loud and insistent, a counterpoint to Cameron's oppressive murmurs. Her eyes burned with frustration as she observed him, determined to figure out a way to expose Packer's involvement in her mother's death.

Chapter Sixteen

Unraveling Truths

Following her very public and humiliating breakup with Kirk months earlier, Blair had meticulously flipped the narrative in her favor. Being unapologetic proved to be the ultimate power move. Blair inked a lucrative deal to launch her own fashion and beauty line, *Untouchable by Blair Dupont*. With a blockbuster movie role on the table and high-profile collaborations on the horizon, she wasn't just back—she was *everywhere*.

When Kirk attempted to challenge her in the media, Blair stayed ten steps ahead. Instead of firing back, she strategically aligned herself with influential allies in the industry, ensuring that every door he tried to close on her only led to bigger opportunities.

With the scandal that nearly ruined her career now in the past, she felt it was time to attempt to heal her with relationship with Kirk. If only because they both cherished the son they shared together.

The hallway stretched before Blair like an accusation, each step echoing the inevitable end she'd been avoiding. She paused at the front door of Kirk's penthouse, being there was a cruel reminder of the life they'd once shared. Her hand hovered over the doorknob, a brief moment of hesitation that almost felt like hope. But she knew better. Taking a deep breath, she entered using her key. Kirk was waiting, he knew she was coming. He was sitting on the arm of the sofa with the detached air of someone who'd already moved on. She took in the familiar surroundings. Her eyes lingered, *this might be the last time*, she thought, a silent acknowledgment that hit harder than she'd expected.

He looked up as she walked in, the usual spark in his eyes dimmed by the weight of their history. "Hey," he said, his voice carrying the practiced nonchalance of someone who'd been rehearsing this moment.

Blair sat across from Kirk, trying to calm her nerves.

"So, this is it, huh?" Kirk muttered, sitting down on the sofa.

"You tell me. Can we make this right or am I trying to hold on to something that isn't there anymore?"

He scoffed, shaking his head. "Is that the same question you asked Skee?"

Blair rolled her eyes. "This isn't about Skee. This is about us. I've changed. I'm not the same woman I was when we got together. And you're not the same man. We have to stop pretending."

Kirk exhaled sharply, then finally nodded. "I guess that's that then."

The coldness of his words stung more than she cared to admit, a memento of everything that still lingered between them. There was this silence like an unwelcome third party in the room.

"Let's hit the reset button," he said, interrupting the silence before it grew too heavy. "How have you been?"

"Busy. You know, with work," Blair said in a softer tone.

He nodded, his fingers drumming idly against his knee. "Yeah, you're everywhere these days. I gotta give you your props; what looked like career suicide, you turned into the biggest comeback of the year," he laughed, his tenor filled with a hint of admiration.

"Yeah," she said, a regretful edge creeping into her voice. "I was in survival mode. But I wish it hadn't gotten so ugly between us at times. And you?"

"I wish the same," Kirk replied, his voice tinged with his own regret. "But everything's good. Focusing on Donovan and basketball."

They lapsed back into silence, each searching for the right way to say what they both knew had to be said. Blair watched him carefully, the familiarity of his gestures both comforting and painful.

"It's not easy," she finally spoke, the words coming out in a rush. "Being here. Like this."

Kirk met her gaze, his expression softening. "I know. But it's not like we didn't see it coming."

She felt a pang of sadness, the truth of his statement cutting through her like a cold wind. "I guess I just hoped..."

He shook his head, interrupting gently. "Hoped what, Blair? That we could make it work again?"

"It might sound crazy but yeah," she admitted, the vulnerability in her voice almost undoing her. "I guess so."

He let out a sigh and ran a hand through his short, cropped curls, a habit Blair used to find endearing. Now, it felt like a reminder of how far they'd drifted. "We gave it a shot, a few different times, didn't we? But it's just..."

She nodded, finishing the thought for him. "Not enough."

The gravity of those words enveloped them, oppressive and stifling. They remained quiet, the burden of their choice pressing down like the unyielding summer heat.

"It doesn't have to be messy," Kirk said, his voice filled with an earnestness she hadn't expected. "We can share custody of Donovan. Work out all the details so we don't have to go to court, because I don't want that."

"I don't want that either," she conceded. Blair really stared at Kirk and saw the man she'd loved and the stranger he'd become, both wrapped into one. "You're right, it doesn't have to be messy." A bittersweet smile touched her lips.

He stood, awkwardly, as if unsure whether to hug her or just walk away. "You'll be okay," he said, more statement than question.

She rose to meet him, the moment stretching out like an unfinished sentence. "So will you," she replied, a silent plea for it to be true.

The goodbye was wordless, an exchange of looks that spoke louder than any farewell. Blair gave him one

last glance before turning and walking out, leaving behind the last remnants of what once was. Her heart heavy
but relieved, like a storm that had finally broken. As she
walked down the hallway, the sound of the door closing
behind her was both an ending and a beginning.

Kennedy sat across from Sebastian at an upscale rooftop
restaurant, trying to read the expression on his face. It
had been weeks since her bombshell press conference,
and while the public had responded positively, her personal life had taken a major hit.

"I didn't know if you'd come," she admitted, her
voice a fragile thread that threatened to unravel.

Sebastian attempted a casual shrug, but it came
across as cautious. "Yeah, well," he said, glancing out the
window before meeting her gaze. "I wasn't sure either."

The words lingered between them, fragile and uncertain until Kennedy finally let out a soft breath. "I'm
glad you did."

"Is this your way of making amends?" Sebastian
asked, swirling the whiskey in his glass. "A fancy dinner
and an apology?"

"I don't expect a fancy dinner to fix everything," Kennedy sighed, her eyes reflecting a mix of regret and hope.
"I screwed up, Sebastian. I know that. And I've been trying to figure out how to make things right. I just... I want
to be honest with you. No more secrets. No more lies."

Sebastian's expression was guarded, like someone
approaching a house of cards. He leaned back, considering her words, the slight tension in his shoulders a testa-

ment to the caution that held him in place. "You know in relationships I've always lived by three simple rules, love needs action, trust needs proof and sorry needs change. I'm no longer sure we can have that."

Kennedy ran her fingers along the rim of her glass, gathering her thoughts like delicate bits of porcelain. "I understand why you feel that way and I've been doing a lot of thinking," she said, her voice barely rising above the low hum of conversation around them. "About us. About everything. I know I let you down. I should've come to you before I did that press conference. You felt blindsided."

"Because I was," Sebastian cut her off.

"I know," she said, her voice steadying with conviction. "But I'm willing to do whatever it takes to prove to you that I am sorry, you can trust me and that I sincerely love you."

Sebastian tilted his head, a half-smile playing on his lips, equal parts wistful and skeptical. "You think it's that easy? Just hit reset?"

She shook her head, the urgency in her voice rising. "No, I know it's not easy. I just... I want to try. I want to be better," she said, the admission raw and honest. "And I know I don't deserve it, but I'm hoping we can start over."

Sebastian studied her for a long moment before exhaling. "I won't lie, Kennedy. It's hard for me to trust you after everything. But I do know one thing—you're a fighter. And that's something I've always admired about you."

"Then let me fight for us. But only if we still have a chance." Kennedy watched him, her heart in her throat, each second prolonging out with cruel patience.

"I meant what I said last time," he finally spoke, his

voice quieter now, laden with past hurts and new possibilities. "I don't want to go through that again. I have to know the woman I'm with is my partner and whatever comes our way, we're united in facing it together."

"I promise. I'm a different person now and one of the reasons for that is because I do love you. I don't want to lose you."

He watched her closely, the fragments of old wounds still visible beneath the surface of his calm exterior. His eyes became gentler, yet a trace of uncertainty lingered. "I don't know, Kennedy. I want to believe you but a lot has happened."

"Then let me show you," Kennedy implored.

Something shifted in his expression, the barest hint of belief cutting through the uncertainty. Sebastian hesitated before giving her hand a small squeeze. "Okay. Let's see where this goes. No promises. But I want to try because I love you too."

Kennedy's heart lifted, her breath catching in a moment that felt surreal. "Thank you."

Sebastian reached across the table, his fingers brushing against hers in a gesture that spoke louder than any declaration. "Don't make me regret this," he said, his smile matching hers now.

"I won't," Kennedy replied, a vow as solid as the love they deeply shared.

The late afternoon light filtered through the curtains, casting lazy patterns across the room. Blair was sprawled on her bed, gazing at her phone as she reread Skee's text.

He had invited her to join him on his tour stop in Miami, and now he was asking if she had made up her mind. She wasn't sure she was ready to walk back through that door.

Kirk's image flickered in her thoughts, a recollection she was prepared to release. It was time to embrace a fresh start. What did she have to lose? More crucially, what might she gain?

A surge of excitement shot through her, but doubt soon crept in. Still, Blair considered having some fun would be a welcome distraction after her and Kirk permanently ended their relationship. Additionally, it might provide her with an opportunity to delve deeper into Packer.

Blair sat up, running a hand through her hair, trying to smooth out the tangles in her thoughts. Miami. The word buzzed in her mind like an intoxicating melody. It was the kind of decision that felt reckless and thrilling, the kind she used to make before she became a mother and part of the NBA WAGs club.

She grabbed a pillow, hugging it to her chest as if it could contain the mixed emotions spilling out of her. "Stop overthinking it," Blair muttered to herself, the sound of her own voice breaking the heavy silence. She took a deep breath, feeling the weight of her indecision lifting as she made up her mind. Blair tapped out a short reply "I'm in."

Chapter Seventeen

Deadly Decisions

Darcy sat at the kitchen table; her fingers wrapped tightly around a glass of tequila. Across from her, Michael paced back and forth, his face twisted in fury.

"You did what?!" he bellowed, his fists clenched at his sides.

Darcy took a steady sip of her drink, unbothered by his rage. "I signed the papers, Michael. Glitz Inc. belongs to Kennedy again. It's over."

Michael slammed his hand down on the counter, making the glassware rattle. "You spineless bitch! Do you know what you've done? After everything I built, you just handed it back to her?"

Darcy scoffed, standing up to face him. "What you

built? You mean what I built while you were running your law firm. Let's be real, Michael. This was never about the company—it was about your ego. About your pathetic obsession with Blair and how she left you for Kirk. You wanted to take something from her, and Kennedy was the perfect pawn."

Michael's face darkened, his breathing ragged. "You're making a big mistake."

Darcy took a step closer, her voice icy. "No, Michael. The only mistake I made was believing that if I was the perfect girlfriend who kissed your ass, you would realize that I'm the right woman for you, not that pseudo actress model. But you refuse to accept that you're just not her type. She went from an NBA player to now a rap super-star. Clearly, Blair doesn't like men who wear overpriced designer suits," she snarled as she finished her tequila in one swift gulp, promptly reaching to refill her glass, only to find the bottle empty. Determined to keep numbing her pain with alcohol, she staggered towards the kitchen.

Michael lunged at her, grabbing her arm with bruis-ing force. "You're not walking away from this. You don't get to just—"

In a blur, Darcy yanked away, her glass slipping from her fingers shattering on the floor. "You don't run me any-more Michael, I'm done. Now fuck off!"

"I run everything!" Michael roared, as he advanced, the shattered glass crackling under his pricey loafers. "Nobody crosses me, especially not some nothing ass woman like you."

Darcy felt the air closing in, the wide space of the kitchen suddenly tight, suffocating. The scent of fresh orchids on the center island mingled with the distinct bite of tequila. Her hand trembled as she reached for the polished block beside her, fingers closing around the smooth handle of a kitchen knife. It was long, gleaming, more weapon than utensil.

Michael's eyes widened when he saw the blade, but he didn't stop. "You think a knife is going to scare me? You're even more pathetic than I thought."

"Just stay the fuck away from me, Michael. I'm serious." Darcy's voice wavered slightly, a crack in her defiant armor.

"Give it up and drop the knife. You're too inept and weak to follow through anything," he taunted, extending a hand as though he could make the knife disappear by sheer force.

She held the knife up, a silent warning between them, but Michael kept coming, rage in his eyes, in his every movement. Darcy's skin tingled uncomfortably as she tightened her grip on the handle. She felt her own pulse hammering in her ears, drowning out any logic or doubts.

"You destroyed my life, Michael!" she shouted, taking a step back as he closed in, the sharp edge of the countertop pressing into her spine. "You never loved me, and you never deserved my loyalty."

Their voices rose, colliding like tidal waves. "I warned you," he growled, so close now Darcy could see the small bead of sweat on his temple.

"Stop it," she pleaded, her control slipping with each word.

Michael made the fatal mistake of underestimating just how far Darcy had deteriorated. There was one lunge too many.

The knife flashed in the bright overhead light, a silver arc through the air. It found its mark, the movement swift and precise. In a state of complete inebriation and acting on impulse, without hesitation, she plunged it into his chest. For a moment, Michael just stood there, stunned, eyes locked on Darcy's, searching, disbelieving. He gasped, a choked sound that stopped all time in the sterile, silent kitchen.

She didn't move. She couldn't. The knife remained in her hand, wet with guilt and crimson. Darcy finally let it go as Michael stumbled backward, gripping the handle protruding from his chest, each step an eternity, each breath a struggle. The sleek, polished floor rose up to meet him as he collapsed, his legs giving way, his protests silenced. The blood spread across his pristine white shirt.

Darcy watched, her own breath coming in short, ragged bursts. She saw Michael's body crumpled and small, the marble countertop dug into her back, grounding her in the shocking reality of what she'd done.

His lips moved, a soundless accusation, a final plea lost in the space between them. Then nothing. Just the cold silence of the kitchen, swallowing the echoes of violence, of desperation, of choices that couldn't be unmade.

After the initial shock faded, Darcy hovered over Michael, as if to inspect her handiwork, her breath coming in sharp bursts. "I told you," she whispered. "I'm done."

Diamond was in her office, going over a new set of proofs when the door opened sharply, and Marcus walked in. He was wearing a sleek charcoal grey suit. The clean lines and modern sharp cut, accentuated his athletic frame, highlighting his youthful energy yet confident, sophisticated flair. It was the kind of attire that demanded attention, but in an understated way. Not only did he have style Marcus also had the kind of infectious smile that dared you to believe in happy endings. Diamond couldn't help but wish they had reconnected at a different time in her life.

As the door closed with a click behind him, his presence shifted the atmosphere in the room from professional to charged immediately.

"Surprise visit?" Diamond asked, trying for casual but unable to mask her fondness for him.

Marcus didn't answer, not with words. He closed the distance between them, and the tension in her shoulders melted away as he pulled her to her feet. Their lips met in a kiss that was more than hello, more than anything she was ready to admit. It was passion and memory and everything they couldn't have but took anyway.

For a long moment, the city disappeared. The skyline, the office, the sketches—all gone in the depth of that kiss. He had a way of literally taking her breath away and she didn't want to give it up.

"If I keep kissing you, I'll never make my deadline," she said with an awkward smile, sitting down.

Marcus took a seat across from her desk. The temptations, the pull between them—hung heavy in the air. He reached out, his fingers brushing against hers. "Diamond, you know how we feel about each other, so whatever's on your mind, you can tell me," he said, sensing something was wrong.

She closed her eyes, swallowing the lump in her throat. "I don't even know where to start. I mean we've already crossed the line, so there's no going back."

Marcus stood and walked around the desk, gently cupping her face. "I don't want to go back. I want us to keep moving forward. Choose what makes you happy."

Once again for a moment, Diamond let herself lean into him. Let herself feel the warmth, the comfort, the escape. Their lips met in a slow, lingering kiss, filled with every unspoken word between them.

But then, she pulled away. Diamond broke it with a steady hand, pressing her palm to his chest and stepping back, reclaiming her breath, her control.

"I have to salvage my marriage," she whispered. "Which means we can't do this anymore. And we can't work together."

He searched her eyes, looking for the answer he wanted. "You don't mean that—"

"Yes, I do. I care about you, much more than I should. But I have a husband and a family that's worth fighting for," she said, her voice firm and unyielding, but with an edge of pain that was impossible to hide. The words lay between them, a line she was no longer willing to cross.

Marcus watched her, still and silent. Diamond turned away, trying to regain the focus she'd lost the moment he walked in. She tried to act like this wasn't breaking her in ways she didn't want to show.

"It's just for now, you know that, right?" Marcus stated, not wanting to let go.

She hesitated, her resolve cracking ever so slightly. "For now," she repeated, a whisper of doubt in the words.

Then, with more strength than she felt, "I've chosen my husband and my children. I need you to understand."

Marcus nodded, but his eyes were wounded, his hands at his sides, not reaching for her, not willing to fight what she'd already decided. He took a step back, giving her the space she needed, respecting the boundaries she was trying so hard to set.

Diamond repositioned herself, sitting behind the desk like a queen on a throne made of choices. Choices that pained her, that defined what she was willing to sacrifice. She didn't look up, didn't trust herself to say goodbye. Diamond listened as the door clicked shut, as if it were the last page in a story that had only begun or a final period at the end of a sentence, she wasn't ready to finish but must. Diamond allowed herself a small, bittersweet smile, then picked up the pen and got back to work.

Blair arrived in Miami, stepping into a whirlwind of flashing lights and deafening music. Though hesitant to accept Skee's invitation to join him on his tour stop, it was the perfect distraction she needed.

"Baby, I'm glad you're here," Skee said squeezing Blair's hand as security guided them past the velvet rope.

"Me too. Being here with you is exactly where I need to be," she smiled.

"I know this isn't how you wanted to spend your first night in Miami, but since I was paid a small fortune to attend the grand opening, I gotta be here. So, I appreciate you joining me," Skee said, kissing Blair on the lips.

When they entered the strip club, ***Drake's Gimme A Hug*** was booming from the high-definition speakers.

> *Walk in the strip club, damn I missed you hoes, gimme a hug*
> *Gimme a hug, gimme a hug, gimme a hug, gimme a hug*
> *Yeah, I know that you work at the club*
> *Know that these people might judge*
> *But fuck it, you family to us*
> *So come over here and gimme some love*
> *Princess, Gigi, Pooh, Pink, Luxury, y'all*
> *gotta come to the stage*
> *Yeah, come to the stage and show me some love...*

Blair's eyes scanned the extravagant venue. Everything was opulent—red carpet entrance, golden chandeliers, and the finest champagne being poured by models decorated in diamonds. The thick, hot air reeked of sweat and perfume. Girls spun on poles above the crowd, a blur of skin and neon thongs, and a shower of bills rained down in the epileptic light. She sat in the roped-off VIP section with Skee, sipping champagne as she watched the crowd. That's when she saw her, Lyric and realized she was the one hosting the event.

"I'll be right back," she told Skee putting her glass down.

"Babe, where you goin'?" he asked standing up to follow her.

"You stay here. I just need to have a quick word with Lyric," Blair said, placing a reassuring hand on Skee before rushing away.

Lyric, draped in a shimmering silver gown, stood by the bar, her confident posture shifting slightly when she saw Blair's approach. Her large hoop earrings dangled as she tilted her head, observing Blair draw nearer. She wore a smirk like a protective shield, but it cracked as Blair came closer.

Blair shoved her way past a group of giggling women, not caring about the drinks that splashed in their glasses. As she made her way toward her the memory of what she'd learned burned in her mind—Lyric had drugged Cameron. Had manipulated him. Had nearly destroyed Diamond's marriage.

Blair's long black hair whipped behind her, a flag of intent. She had to stop herself from smacking the grin off Lyric's face, but this wasn't the time or place. "You drugged Cameron and then filmed it you dirty bitch!" she shouted, the accusation like a bullet through the music.

Lyric's smirk vanished, and she paused briefly before regaining her composure. "You can't prove shit," she shot back, raising her voice above the noise. She glanced around, her eyes darting to the exits.

"I know you did it," Blair spit, leaning in, her words edged with fury. "Everyone knows. You're a vile, manipulative snake."

Lyric stood her ground, a wall of defiance. She shrugged, playing at indifference, "Oh, sweetheart. That's old news. Find a new insult. Besides, what're you gonna do about it? I ain't scared of you," she hissed dramatically. But Blair saw her flinch.

Nearby, YaYa sat on the plush red couches in the VIP section as the drama was unfolding. She hesitated, eyes shifting between Lyric, Blair and the tiny vial of a lethal drug she should have slipped into Lyric's drink over an hour ago. Yet, she found herself unable to carry out Packer's sinister scheme. She chewed her bottom lip, picked up her phone, and typed out a swift, anxious message: *I can't do it!*

She hovered over the send button, trapped in a moment of indecision, when a dancer slid onto the couch beside her, tossing long 24-inch blonde bundles and sparkling with fake diamonds. "You okay, girl?" the dancer asked, blowing her a kiss as she moved on to the next high roller.

YaYa swallowed, trying to focus. She stared at the phone, then back at the growing scene, her thumb trembling. She finally hit send, but it was too late.

Blair pressed on, not giving an inch. "Your confident facade is crumbling. I see right through your tough girl act. I'm gonna make it my business to use my platform to let everyone know the grimy shit you did because of your thirst for fame," she vowed.

Lyric adjusted her stance, arms crossing tightly over her chest, revealing a noticeable fracture in her poise. "You need to back off," she cautioned, attempting to appear more assertive than she actually felt.

Blair's anger was flaring, their voices rose in rapid-fire exchange, but before the women started laying hands, the energy in the club shifted. The air grew thick with something dangerous. Blair's eyes flickered to the entrance just as Packer burst through the doors, flanked by two burly goons. Their guns were drawn, and the crowd split like oil on water, the panic of bodies scattering in every direction. YaYa jumped to her feet, dropping her phone on the couch as she stared in horror.

"Lyric!" YaYa screamed, pointing toward the intrusion.

Blair's eyes widened as she saw Packer shoving his way through the confusion, the barrel of his gun like an accusation aimed at her. She grabbed Lyric's wrist, her own fear flashing, but Lyric wrenched free, stumbling back.

The scene turned into chaos as Packer charged forward pushing people out of his way. The pulsing music clashed with the screams, creating a soundtrack of pure panic. Girls ran for the dressing room, a bartender ducked behind the counter, and the lights kept flashing, stuttering through the mayhem.

"Get that bitch!" Packer shouted to his goons, his voice rigid.

Lyric spun, losing her bravado as she dashed for the door. Blair made to follow, but the crowd surged around her, a sea of confusion and terror. She was trapped, struggling against the tide of people. The club descended into pandemonium.

Skee, who had been laughing just moments before, turned to see Packer raising the gun, aiming in Blair's direction. His breath caught. He watched Packer's steady, menacing advance, the gun outstretched in his hand, and without a second thought, he leapt forward.

He wasn't thinking—he just moved.

"Blair!" he shouted, lunging toward her just as the shot rang out, louder than the bass, louder than the screams. The impact sent Skee sprawling onto the floor, and a nearby clubgoers drink flying from their hand, shattering on the ground. The music cut off abruptly, leaving only the raw sound of chaos and fear.

Blair screamed in horror as Skee fell. His body jerked violently, his arms wrapping around her as he absorbed the bullet trying to protect her. Blood splattered onto her dress after Skee collapsed in her arms.

Lyric stopped in her tracks, eyes wide with shock as she watched from the open door.

"Somebody call an ambulance!" Blair shouted, crouching over Skee's crumpled form. He lay still, the vibrant lights casting him in shades of red and white. Blood pooled beneath him, stark against the colorful floor.

YaYa grabbed her phone, frantically dialing as tears blurred her vision. "Please, hurry!" she cried into the receiver. She looked at Packer, his expression shifting from triumph to anger as he took in the scene, people screaming and rushing for the exits. He motioned to his goons. They bolted, shoving their way through the stunned crowd to vanish into the night, but bouncers tackled Packer and his henchmen before they could make their grand getaway.

Blair held onto Skee, panic choking her as she pressed her hands against his wound, desperate to stop the bleeding. "Skee! Stay with me! Stay with me," she repeated, a mantra against the mounting dread.

Tears blurred Blair's vision as the chaos of the club swirled around her. Packer was dragged away by security, and Lyric, shaking, took an unsteady step back. But Blair had no time for anything else.

She just held onto Skee, praying he wouldn't die in her arms.

The crowd thinned, people spilling out onto the street, sirens already echoing in the distance. The strobe lights flickered, and the atmosphere heavy with the metallic scent of blood and smoke.

Skee coughed, his eyes fluttering as he tried to focus on Blair. "I told you I'd always have yo' back. You my superstar," he whispered, a small, pained smile ghosting across his lips.

Tears ran down Blair's face as she held on to him, to hope. The club was a wreck around them, a war zone of fallen chairs and broken bottles. The silence was heavy, shattered only by the distant wail of sirens and the faint, desperate sound of Blair's voice.

"Hold on, Skee," she said. "Please, hold on."

Epilogue...Six Months Later

Baller Bitches Reborn

The soothing scent of eucalyptus and lavender at the most exclusive spa in New York only enriched its allure. The gentle sound of water trickling from a nearby fountain mixed with the soft hum of tranquil music, setting the perfect atmosphere for a long-overdue catch-up.

Diamond entered the private lounge first, where the walls of glass were softened by waterfalls, whispering fabrics, and left a swirl of perfume and purpose in her wake. Her long, shimmering coat flowed behind her, catching the ambient light, and she paused to survey the serene luxury with the satisfaction of someone who belonged. Removing her sunglasses, she revealed eyes bright with anticipation and eased herself into the chair, crossing her legs with practiced elegance.

Kennedy followed in heels as high as her spirits, throwing air kisses at the young attendant who scurried to open the door, and sank into a plush leather chair with the comfort of old money. Her hair, an angled ombre lob, with dark roots that gradually transitioned into gorgeous blonde at the tips and gleamed under the soft lights as she tossed it back with an airy laugh. The jangle of designer bracelets punctuated her every move as she joined Diamond, her arrival a crescendo of style and ambition.

Blair arrived last, as always, flicking her eyes and wrists as if in constant judgment, making her way past the low murmur of trophy wives and trust fund babies who decorated the tranquil space. Her hair was pulled back with slick precision, revealing a flawless face that hinted at fatigue and purpose. The cut of her jacket was sharp, her expression sharper, as she took in the room with quick glances. She settled beside her friends and before long, Diamond, Kennedy, and Blair were lounging in plush robes, chatting and catching up with each other.

Diamond leaned back against the massage chair, a blissful smile on her face. pressing one palm against her slightly rounded stomach, she was beaming and declared, "I can finally say it—I'm happy. While we were on vacation... well, we weren't exactly careful. I'm pregnant again!"

Kennedy gasped, reaching for Diamond's hand. "Congratulations!"

Blair, despite the sadness still lingering in her eyes, managed a genuine smile. "That's amazing, Diamond. You deserve this happiness."

Diamond caressed her belly, her excitement undeniable. "After everything, it feels dreamlike, but Cameron and I are stronger than ever. We renewed our vows in Fiji, on the beach at sunset. It was simple and perfect." Her eyes glistened with remembered joy. "Everything feels right now, and our baby is a fresh start for us."

Kennedy lifted her champagne flute, a proud glint in her eyes. "Speaking of fresh starts, Glitz Inc. is thriving. Business is booming, and despite all the chaos, I managed to come out on top. And..." Kennedy beamed, flicking her fingers to send the diamond dancing in the light. "Sebastian finally put a ring on it," she declared. "He popped the question last week," flashing her left hand, showcasing a dazzling diamond.

Both Diamond and Blair beamed in delight. "No way!" Diamond clapped her hands. "That's incredible! I knew you'd reel him back in," Diamond said with a wink. "Sebastian didn't stand a chance."

Kennedy let out a musical laugh, her delight effervescent. "You know how men are," she said, with a dismissive wave. "They need to think it's their idea." She glanced at her ring, a sparkle catching her eye. "On a serious note, it took some time, but our love prevailed. No more secrets, no more lies," Kennedy smiled, twirling her newly acquired engagement ring between two fingers, nodding in enthusiastic approval.

"The ring is stunning, and I'm genuinely thrilled for you and Sebastian. I can't wait for the wedding!" Diamond exclaimed.

Kennedy agreed. "After everything we went through, I wasn't sure if he'd ever fully trust me again. But we worked through it. He saw me at my lowest, and he still chose me. That's real love."

Blair stared out over the terrace, where the glow

of the city blurred the line between sky and street. She reclined with a measured sigh, crossing her arms in a relaxed manner while tapping her nails against the glass-topped table as she observed them both. "Sounds like everything's falling into place," she said, the slightest edge to her tone. "For some of us."

Blair then went quiet, the echoes of their joy amplifying her own sense of loss. Her eyes drifted to the fountain, following the gentle cascade as if it held answers, she could not voice.

"Blair, you know you can share anything with us. Even though we're celebrating my engagement and Diamond's pregnancy, we're also here to listen to you if you need us," Kennedy said warmly.

"I know, I just need to figure out what I want," Blair remarked, her vulnerability contrasting sharply against the backdrop of their certainty.

Diamond and Kennedy exchanged knowing glances. "Things will turn around, Blair," Diamond said, her voice full of assurance. "They did for me."

Blair exhaled, her fingers absentmindedly tracing the rim of her champagne glass. "I'm so happy for you all, I really am. You both deserve happiness. But I'm still struggling with Skee's loss," she admitted, her words hanging heavy in the air. "He should be here. It's painful knowing he lost his life trying to protect me."

The conversation stilled, a silent respect for what had been lost. Kennedy reached over, squeezing Blair's hand. "We're here for you, but please know none of this was your fault. Justice is on its way. Packer and his crew are behind bars, destined to languish in prison not only for Skee but also for Diamond's mother."

Diamond nodded solemnly. "I still can't believe how everything played out. I had lost hope that anyone would ever be arrested for my mother's murder. I'm grateful she will finally receive justice."

"We are too," Kennedy and Blair both chimed in. They understood the impact her mother's murder had on her and hoped that Diamond could finally start to recover from her grief.

Diamond relaxed into her chair, letting the outside world fade away. "Cameron has truly stepped up and been my rock. We're flying to Aspen next weekend," she said, her voice a ribbon of possibility. "It's his idea, but you know me—I never say no to the mountains."

Kennedy raised her eyebrows, a flash of envy and admiration. "I should let you plan our honeymoon," she said, only half-joking. "Sebastian's thinking St. Tropez, but maybe we'll do both, go there and you plan our honeymoon."

"I'm game. You should never limit yourself." Diamond laughed, the sound like champagne bubbles.

Blair watched them, their joy was infectious and brought a gleam to her eyes. "St. Tropez is a far cry from the hood," she noted with a hint of irony in her voice.

Kennedy's laugh joined Diamond's, a duet of triumph over circumstance. "And we're never going back," Kennedy declared, tapping her ring with renewed emphasis.

"Amen! I'm really in a great place right now," Diamond said with a smile, resting her hand on her stomach. "You all don't need to worry about me. But Blair, I am concerned about you. You've lost two exes in such violent ways. Skee and Michael."

"Darcy killing Michael still has me shook," Kennedy admitted. "She's sitting in a jail cell awaiting trial, leaving the whole world in shock. But one thing's for sure—she's never getting out."

"I'm not sure I'll ever recover from witnessing Skee's death right before my eyes, but truthfully, I'm not shocked about Michael. No way am I trying to defend Darcy's actions, as she is undoubtedly a dangerous woman, but Michael could be incredibly cold. There were numerous times I wanted to permanently remove him from my life," Blair divulged.

"Luckily you managed to do that without resorting to murder," Kennedy quipped.

"No rush, but when you're ready to get back on the dating scene, I'd love to play matchmaker," Diamond volunteered.

Blair let out a deep breath and straightened her shoulders. "For now, I'm staying single, focusing on co-parenting with Kirk, and my acting career. And guess what? I just landed one of the leading roles in what is supposed to be a new movie franchise. "

That's fuckin' amazing!" Kennedy and Diamond cheered, raising their glasses in a toast. "To new beginnings. To survival. And to winning!" Diamond praised taking a sip of her sparkling apple cider.

As Kennedy drained the last of her drink, the ice settled with a soft clink, admiration lighting her features. "That's why I love you, Diamond," she declared. "You always know what you want."

"And I go for it," Diamond replied, her tone decisive. "Nothing will stop any of us and that's a direct order." She glanced at Blair, a subtle invitation lingering in her gaze.

Kennedy laughed, the sound unguarded and full. "I love it when you get bossy," she said, playfully.

Blair gave a small smile, the first one that truly lit up her face. She joined in, their flutes clinking in a harmonious nod to their shared past. "And to perseverance," she added, a hint of hope mingled with careful optimism.

The flowers at the center of the table drew their attention, a delicate arrangement vibrant with potential. Diamond touched one of the petals, her fingers light and deliberate. "We've endured a lot, but we survived it and are blessed for many reasons, one of which is having each other."

"Indeed, we do, and that calls for one last toast!" Kennedy exclaimed with enthusiasm.

As they clinked glasses, the sun cast a golden glow over them. They had been tested, betrayed, and nearly broken, but they had come out stronger. The past would always be a part of them, but the future? The future was theirs to own.

The End

A KING PRODUCTION

Bitch

The Story Of Precious Cummings

MOVIE EDITION

A Novel

JOY DEJA KING

Started From The Bottom

Coming from nothing and having nothing are two different things. Yeah, I came from nothing, but I was determined to have it all. And how couldn't I?

I exploded into this world when hood rich wasn't an afterthought, but the only thought. You turn on the television or go on social media and every nigga is iced out with an exotic whip, surrounded by a bitch in a G-string, bundles down to her ass, poppin' that booty. So, the chicks in videos were dropping it like it's hot for the rappers, singers and athletes, while the bitches around my way were dropping it for our own superstars. Dealing with a street nigga on a legendary drug kingpin status was like being Beyonce herself on Jigga Man's arm. A bitch like me was thirsty for that. I'd been on some

type of hustle since I was in pampers. I grew up in the grimiest Brooklyn projects. It was worse than being in prison because you knew there was something better out there; you just didn't know how to get it. You never saw green grass or flowers blooming. Instead of looking up to teachers, lawyers, or doctors, you worshipped the local drug dealers who hustled to survive and escape their existence. Even as a little girl, I knew I wanted more out of life. Somehow hustling was in my blood.

First, I hustled for my moms' attention because she was too busy turning tricks to pay me any mind. I never knew who my daddy was, so while my mom was fucking in her bedroom, I would wait outside the door with my legs crossed, holding my favorite teddy bear in one arm as I sucked my thumb. When the tricks would come out, I would look at them with puppy-dog eyes and ask, "Are you, my daddy?" The question would freak them out so badly they'd toss me a few dollars so I would shut the fuck up.

One day when I was five, my mother was looking for something in my drawers, she came across a bunch of fives and tens and some twenties. The total was five hundred and some change. Of course, she wanted to know where all the money came from. When I told her that the money came from her business clients (that's what my mom called them), she lit up. She tossed me up in the air and said, "Baby, you my good luck charm. I knew one day you'd make me some money."

On that rare occasion she showed me mad love. As young as I was, I equated my mother's newfound interest in me with love. From that moment on, I learned how to hustle for my moms' attention, by providing her with money.

Somehow, my moms' customers never messed with or tried to fondle me. I think it's because even as a little girl I had this darkness in my eyes, that said, "Don't fuck wit' me."

By the time I was fifteen with all the tricks my mom's pulled, we were still dead ass broke, living in the projects. She couldn't save a dime because with hooking comes drugging and my mom's stayed high. I guess that's all you can do to escape the nightmare of having all types of nasty, greasy fat motherfuckers pounding your back out every damn day. The characters that I saw coming in and out of our apartment were enough to make me want to sew up my pussy so nobody could get between my legs, but my mother would soon change all that.

One day, I was sitting at home watching a weekly vlog on YouTube from one of my favorite social media influencers. She was doing beauty maintenance and self-care. I was completely caught up that I almost didn't hear my mother's bedroom door open. I heard the floor squeak and immediately turned off the television. Without a word, I started giving the living room a lick and a promise. I emptied several full ashtrays, picked up the dirty glasses scattered about the floor

and wiped off the cocktail table.

Out of the corner of my eye, I watched my mother stare at me for a few minutes. She had the strangest look on her face. She was holding a bottle of whiskey in one hand and a cigarette in the other. My mother was only 33 but living a reckless life filled with drugs and heavy drinking had taken its toll. With unkept hair, poor hygiene, and a nasty disposition, most of the time I couldn't stand being around her. There was no trace of the once curvy beauty that every hood chick envied. Her once long, wavy hair was now thin and straggly. The one-time ghetto queen was just a bag of bones that you wouldn't even recognize unless you stared deeply into the green eyes she inherited from her father.

It was the middle of the afternoon, and she was just waking up, still wearing her dingy nightgown, blowing smoke in the air. She held on tightly to her cig-arette, staring at me as if I was a reminder of what she used to be in her prime.

"Precious, you sure are growing up to be a pretty girl." I stayed silent and continued picking up clothes that were scattered on the floor and then started sweeping. "Didn't you hear what yo' mama said?"

"Yes, I heard you."

"Well, you betta say thank you."

"Thank you, ma."

"You welcome, baby."

My mother walked over to the couch and sat down with her legs spread open. She took one last long pull from her cigarette and put it out in the ashtray. She then took a swig from the whiskey bottle. The alcohol was spilling down her chin.

"Baby, you know that your mother is getting up there in age. I can't put it down like I used to. So baby, I was thinking maybe you need to start helping me out a little more."

Her comment made me pause and frown up my face. "Help you out more how? I basically give you my whole paycheck."

"Like I said, yo' mama can't put it down like I used to."

That bullshit made me stop sweeping the floor and I stared directly in my mother's eyes.

"What does any of that have to do wit' me? I barely go to school as it is because what was supposed to be a parttime job at the car detailing shop is more like fulltime. Damn near every cent I make, goes in your pocket to pay bills."

"Baby, that little job you got ain't bringing home no money. It's just enough to maintain. I'm talking about getting a real job."

I started sweeping the floor again wanting to ignore the foolishness coming out her mouth.

"Ma, I'm fifteen. It's only so many jobs I can get and so much money I can make. My boss not even supposed to give me all the hours she has me doing at the shop. That's why she pays me off the books."

"Precious, as pretty as you are you can be making

thousands of dollars."

"Doing what? What job you know is going to pay a fifteen-year-old high school student thousands of dollars?"

"The oldest profession in the book...sex."

"You said that as if you asking me to do something as innocent as baking cookies for a living. You done lost yo' damn mind. What you tryna be now—my pimp!"

"You betta watch yo' mouth, little girl. I'm yo' mama. Don't forget that."

"Don't you forget it! You must have if you asking me to sell my ass so I can take care of you."

"Not me—us. Shit, I took care of yo' ass for the last fifteen years. Breaking my back and wearing out my pussy to provide us with a good life."

"This is what you call a good life?" I twirled the wooden handle of the broom around the living room as I looked at the cluttered two-bedroom apartment. The hardwood floors were heavily scratched with a few roaches crawling near the entrance to the kitchen. Visible holes in the walls and decaying window frames with cracks in the glass. My mother stood up real defiant like and pointed her finger at me.

"You listen here, a lot of these children around this way don't even have a place to stay. It might not be much to yo' ungrateful ass but it's mine."

"That's a lie. You don't even own this raggedy-ass apartment." We stared each other down for a few moments because I wasn't budging. "Sorry to disappoint you, but I'm not following in your footsteps by selling my pussy to some low-down niggas for money," I made clear then shrugged my shoulders brushing the bullshit off.

"Well then you betta start looking for someplace to live, 'cause I can't support both of us."

"You tryna tell me you would put me out on the streets!"

"You ain't leaving me a choice, Precious. If you can't bring home some extra money, then I'll have to rent out your bedroom to pay the bills."

"Who gon' pay for that piece of shit of a room?"

"Listen, I ain't 'bout to sit up here and argue wit' you. Either you start bringing home some money or find another place to live. It's up to you. But if you don't give me a thousand dollars by the first of the month, I need you out by the second."

"How the fuck am I supposed to come up wit' a thousand dollars by the first of the month?"

"I told you. You betta start using what's between your legs." My trifling mother then cut her eyes at my vagina before her skeletal body disappeared into her dungeon of a bedroom. She was practically sentencing me to the homeless shelter. There was no way I could give her a thousand dollars a month unless I dropped out of high school and worked fulltime at the detail shop. But what made this so fucked up was this had nothing to do with the monthly bills because she had subsidized housing and received plenty of other help from the government. My mother basically wanted me to pay for her out-of-control drug habit.

Because the street life had beaten my mother, she wanted to beat me over the head with bullshit. But I refused to let that happen. I would hustle up that money, but I would do it my way. I was going to pick and choose who was able to play between my legs. My job at the car detailing shop was the perfect place for me to start. Nothing but top-of-the-line hustlers parlayed through, and one of them would be mine.

ORDER FORM

Name:

Address:

City/State:

Zip:

QUANTITY	TITLES	PRICE	TOTAL
	Bitch	$17.99	
	Bitch Reloaded	$17.99	
	The Bitch Is Back	$17.99	
	Queen Bitch	$17.99	
	Last Bitch Standing	$17.99	
	Superstar	$17.99	
	Ride Wit' Me	$17.99	
	Ride Wit' Me Part 2	$17.99	
	Stackin' Paper	$17.99	
	Trife Life To Lavish	$17.99	
	Trife Life To Lavish II	$17.99	
	Stackin' Paper II	$17.99	
	Rich or Famous	$17.99	
	Rich or Famous Part 2	$17.99	
	Rich or Famous Part 3	$17.99	
	Bitch A New Beginning	$17.99	
	Mafia Princess Part 1	$17.99	
	Mafia Princess Part 2	$17.99	
	Mafia Princess Part 3	$17.99	
	Mafia Princess Part 4	$17.99	
	Mafia Princess Part 5	$17.99	
	Boss Bitch	$17.99	
	Baller Bitches Vol. 1	$17.99	
	Baller Bitches Vol. 2	$17.99	
	Baller Bitches Vol. 3	$17.99	
	Bad Bitch	$17.99	
	Still The Baddest Bitch	$17.99	
	Power	$17.99	
	Power Part 2	$17.99	
	Drake	$17.99	
	Drake Part 2	$17.99	
	Female Hustler	$17.99	
	Female Hustler Part 2	$17.99	

QUANTITY	TITLES	PRICE	TOTAL
	Female Hustler Part 3	$17.99	
	Female Hustler Part 4	$17.99	
	Female Hustler Part 5	$17.99	
	Female Hustler Part 6	$17.99	
	Princess Fever "Birthday Bash"	$6.00	
	Nico Carter The Men Of The Bitch Series	$17.99	
	Bitch The Beginning Of The End	$17.99	
	Supreme...Men Of The Bitch Series	$17.99	
	Bitch The Final Chapter	$17.99	
	Stackin' Paper III	$17.99	
	Men Of The Bitch Series And The Women Who Love Them	$17.99	
	Coke Like The 80s	$17.99	
	Baller Bitches The Reunion Vol. 4	$17.99	
	Stackin' Paper IV	$17.99	
	The Legacy	$17.99	
	Lovin' Thy Enemy	$17.99	
	Stackin' Paper V	$17.99	
	The Legacy Part 2	$17.99	
	Assassins - Episode 1	$12.99	
	Assassins - Episode 2	$12.99	
	Assassins - Episode 3	$12.99	
	Bitch Chronicles	$40.00	
	So Hood So Rich	$17.99	
	Stackin' Paper VI	$17.99	
	Female Hustler Part 7	$17.99	
	Toxic...	$12.99	
	Stackin' Paper VII	$17.99	
	Sugar Babies...	$12.99	
	Deadly Divorce...	$12.99	
	The Legacy Part 3	$17.99	
	BITCH The Story of Precious Cummings	$17.99	
	Mastermind...	$12.99	
	Stackin' Paper VIII	$17.99	
	Stackin' Paper Holiday	$12.99	
	Mastermind 2...	$12.99	
	Baller Bitches Vol. 5	$17.99	

Shipping/Handling (Via Priority Mail) $9.85 1-3 Books, $18.40 4-10 Books. For 11 or more $24.75.
Total: $_____FORMS OF ACCEPTED PAYMENTS: Certified or government issued checks and money Orders, all mail in orders take 5-7 Business days to be delivered